Christmas *in* Oberammergau

R.J. Henne
&
J.E. Westerfield

PublishAmerica
Baltimore

First printing

Hardcover 978-1-4512-7477-6
Softcover 978-1-4512-7478-3
PUBLISHED BY PUBLISHAMERICA, LLLP
www.publishamerica.com
Baltimore

Printed in the United States of America

DEDICATION

This children's story is dedicated to all those who open their hearts and homes to foster care, and to adoptive parents whose hearts are big enough to include a child, not of their own, in need of a home. These certainly are special people.

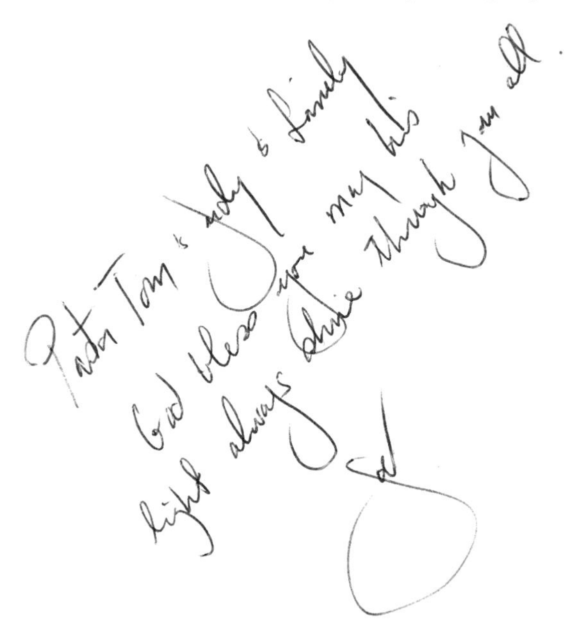

ACKNOWLEDGMENTS

To Sheri Westerfield, editor. She lives in Jacksonville, Il. with Joel and their dogs, Heidi and Zoey. Sheri is my eyes and sounding board during the process of creating my books for publication.

To Shelley Brown, book illustrator, who lives with her husband and one child at home, in Decatur, Il. She is a gifted artist, and created all the drawings for "Christmas in Oberammergau."

To my Lord and Saviour, who gave me the gift of story telling.

Table of Contents

PRELUDE

Christmas in Oberammergau is characterized as a children's story, but, honestly, all ages can relate to this love story. We all experience love in all forms. Love for our parents, love for our spouse, love for our children, our first love that sticks in our memory forever, and the love for our creator. We always hold dear to our heart the unconditional love of a pet we might have had growing up. This is a love story about a very special family who opened their hearts and home to three orphan children at a time when they were looking forward to retirement, after having raised their own children on the family farm and were facing an empty nest. But, God had other plans for them. This is an inspirational story that will tug at your heartstrings. The Deterdings go on an unforgettable journey to find their roots in the land of their ancestors, in Germany. This particular Christmas would prove to be the best they ever had.

ALL POETRY IN THIS BOOK IS ORIGINAL AND COMPOSED BY JOEL E. WESTERFIELD

"Christmas in Oberammergau" Written by R.J. Henne and J.E. Westerfield.

I gave of my money, I gave of my time.
I gave of my body, I gave of my mind.
I gave of my spirit, I gave of my soul.
I gave it all freely and felt the love flow.
No reward did I ask, no fame for my deed,
Yet as much as I gave, so much more I received.

Prelude:

We here in the midwest farming community of Cracker's Bend enjoy the four seasons; Spring that brings new life with the budding of the trees, bushes, and shrubs, the flowers anxiously waiting to peek out of the earth to meet the sunshine and the rain, the grass-covered pastures along clear streams, and long, winding, country roads. It's time for plowing, planting the seed, and putting in our vegetable garden.

The Summer heat slows the body down, seeking a cool place. The living things thirst for a drink of a gentle rain. The farmers are in the field cultivating, and praying for a rain to nourish the young plants. Mom is out gathering fresh vegetables to prepare for our healthy meals. The canning will soon start, to stock up the root cellar and pantry shelves for the winter to come.

Late August, the corn stalks are drying in the fields, and the soy beans, along with the wheat, are turning yellow. Different breezes are felt in September; warm in the daytime, and cool at night, reminding us to bring along a light jacket or sweater.

When October is reached, the lazy summer is over, and there

is plenty to do on the farm. Harvest time is the reward for all of the hard work put into the growing season. We will have to hurry and get the harvest out; stored before the snow flies and the ground hardens. The vegetable garden is bare now; it's bounty put up in mason jars.

Now the last grain is out, the fields are left with stubble, and it's time to celebrate! Look up in the sky to see the full, blood-red harvest moon hanging high and huge over radiant bonfires. As family, friends, and neighbors gather in, they delight over sizzling hot wieners on fork-like sticks, along with gooey hands trying to fit big, blackened, luscious, sticky marshmallows into little mouths. Giggling children with wide, sparkling eyes are in play as adults sit on hay bales around the warm fire, reminiscing. Before the evening is ended we all will load into the straw-covered wagon pulled by the tractor for a hay ride!

Cold rains are expected to come in late October, bringing down the brightly colored leaves of fall. God is preparing the branches for snowy winter attire as leaves are burned up in huge piles. Craft fairs in small surrounding towns are so much fun on sunny, fall days, and the Deterdings will make their yearly trip over to Mr. Lincoln's New Salem State Park. During candle-lit walks through log cabins wood is burning from chimneys, and people are dressed in period costumes, making delectable treats for all the visitors. It's a wonderful way to start the holiday season.

November brings gray skies warning the migrating birds to prepare for their long journey south. Watch closely, for nature tells us that changes are coming soon and we should get prepared. Thanksgiving Day comes rolling around, time for family to gather at the dining room table. A feast is prepared, praising the Lord for His divine help, and, thankful for what we have accomplished that year, let the celebrating begin—the holiday season has begun.

The old man with crystal clear, wind-blown hair, and long, icicle-frozen beard waits a little longer. His knowing, wise old eyes are brilliant as a morning sunrise. With a long, flowing, snowy-white robe, he now sits on his lofty throne as far north as you can reach. Sometimes he is referred to as "Jack Frost", but normally he is called "Winter."

In some parts he anxiously waits for the beautiful Aurora Borealis (Queen of the Northern Lights). Mysteriously she appears, swirling, dancing around in colorful, symmetrical designs, tantalizing those fortunate to take in her rare show of illumination. Wisconsin, Michigan, the Pacific Northwest, and Alaska are use to her frequent visitations, but only on rare occasions is she seen this far south. For those of us who make our home in midwest Illinois, it is truly a phenomenon.

Chapter 1

"Four Seasons"

Horace Deterding and his wife of 55 years, lifetime citizens of "The Bend", farmers by occupation, retired now, sit out in their porch swing just about every late evening while darkness is approaching. They are content, relaxing, gazing out over their farmland they spent a lifetime working, carving their livelihood from. The calming sounds of the night in late fall, rustling leaves high up in the old maple trees grace the lawn that now lies peaceful with their spirit. The noise of crickets rubbing their hind legs together can be annoying; an irritating noise, but the Deterdings are used to it, and find it kind of comforting. The bullfrogs down on Big Indian Creek are also making it known they, too, are around. A shooting star to wish upon darts across the sky, then burns out before it hits the ground. This is all part of the life of a farmer and a farmer's wife.

The Deterding family originated in a village in West Germany, Oberammergau. Although today they are considered "modern day farmers," it hasn't always been that way. Farming is a trade; a craft taught in the family and handed down through the generations of strong men whose passion was to till and tend the ground, and in doing so stayed close to their creator.

Long ago, their grandparents and parents tended this very ground, farming with horses. Walking behind a horse and wooden plow, they planted the crop close together to get the most yield. Carrying a burlap bag on the shoulder, they spread the seed by hand. Most farms were not over 40 acres, around 150 on average. Shucking corn was done by hand while walking beside a wagon. That method of farming is gone forever.

They were frugal people, and lived simple lives. Their cooking and heating came from the wood they chopped themselves to keep the wood cook stove and heating stove going through the bitter winter season and cold springs. The summer heat was endured with the help of a wide open, or screened-in door, and windows raised up high, hoping for any breeze to filter through—not like now-days with central heat and air-conditioning being common.

The farmer's wife's job has also changed through the years. They used to raise their own food, and everything possible was made from scratch. Her sole job was taking care of her home and family. Meal time, the family was expected at the table, and grace was said, thanking the Lord for their bounty. Gathering eggs and slopping the hogs were some of the women's daily work. They milked the cows, providing fresh milk, cream, and butter, and, if enough was left over, buttermilk or cottage cheese was squeezed out from cheesecloth. The delicious, creamy curds were an added treat to the meal. Butchering was done in the winter. Meat, prepared with salt brine and hickory, was hung up in the smoke house to cure.

Clothes were handmade on the old, peddle sewing machine, washed on a washboard, then hung outside on a clothesline in the sun to dry. Lye soap was made from animal fat, not only for washing clothes and cleaning, but for their Saturday night baths.

Making their living off the land and raising their families was not easy. Being dependent on each other caused them to be close-knit and responsible. Chores had to be done every single day regardless of the weather. Taking care of your children and husband was your priority as a farmers wife. Today many wives work outside the home; their jobs / occupations are in town. Things are different now than those of their parents and grandparents. Now a farmer's wife's life is not much different from those who live in the city.

Horace and Sylvia have never been on a vacation in their entire life, but that is about to change this year. Their grown children, Hilda, Moreen, Tabitha, and Luke surprised them—on their 55th anniversary they have convinced them to travel with the entire family back to their roots, to Germany—to cobblestone streets and quaint, thatched roof cottages painted with interesting beautiful murals within small villages where the main occupation is that of wood carving; a craft handed down through generations. So, come Dec. 22nd, they will be boarding a plane for the first time, and spending Christmas in Oberammergau.

But, for now Horace is content to just sit, about every night through the summer and fall months, out in the old porch swing on his farm, watching the sun go down over his fields of corn and soy beans. Since he was born and raised on this old farm, where his grandparents had laid claim and his parents made their living as well, he could never imagine living anywhere else. His son, Luke, has taken over the hardest work, but, Horace is still active, well aware the world around him is changing to high technology, and the time is coming to hand the farm over to the next generation.

Chapter 2

"They Found Contentment Near The Corn And Soy Bean Fields."

Horace finds peace and contentment here among the corn, soy beans, and wheat fields he has known all his life. As he sits with his arms affectionately around his lovely wife of many years, they enjoy these quiet moments here on the farm, the evening sounds are so soothing to the soul. They may discuss the events of the day, or say nothing at all, just sitting back and watching the show overhead performed by the Universal Production Company, produced and directed by The Creator Himself.

A car may pass by and honk it's horn; a neighborly recognition. They think it's their neighbors, the Goodpasture family, or possibly the Boogles. They smile and wave back, for everyone knows one another in these parts, and that is a comforting feeling. The Boogle family's ancestors who came to America in the early 1800's, to Ellis Island, were early settlers from Oberammergau, also.

The wind picked up, and Sylvia shivered, rubbing her arms. A cold chill penetrated through to the bones, calling for a sweater or light jacket. Horace picked up his denim jacket lying over the back of the swing, and draped it around his wife's shoulders. A heavy frost will most certainly be evident by the early morning dawn.

October's frosty nights around these parts bring vibrant colors of yellows, bronzes, and scarlet reds, not only in the shedding leaves but in the golden rod and sumac plants covering the pastures and along roadsides. The bittersweet vines cling heavily to the fences, draping to the ground. They will soon be gathered to make lovely fall and winter bouquets. Fall is the most beautiful time of the year.

Finally, giving it up for the night, sleepy-eyed, they climb the stairs together, hand-in-hand, to their bedroom. Turning on the light in the room, Horace fondly recalls memories of the first time he brought his bride to this house of his ancestors, and of how poor they had been when they first started their life together. Their farm equipment, even to their car and furniture, had been used or borrowed. Back then, every farm was small, just making enough to put a roof over their heads and food for the table.

Their life had been good. God blessed them with four wonderful children who brought laughter, but most of all, love, into their home. Family has meant everything to Horace. His father died instantly in a train accident when Horace was eleven. That morning, he had been riding with his grandfather in the grain truck. They were following his father, close behind his tractor hauling a wagon full of shelled corn to the elevator. His father's old John Deer tractor stalled on the unguarded railroad tracks. He never had a chance.

The horrific tragedy caused young Horace to have nightmares for many years. Being the only boy in the family, he was taught to take on responsibilities early in life. He, his mother, and baby sister, Gilda, stayed on the farm, and the help of their grandparents, in-laws, neighbors and friends got them through the rough years. That all made him very conscious of having enough money, leaving a lasting impression, so that when he grew up he would work hard and never be poor again.

Sylvia was already under the comforter when he came out of the bathroom dressed for bed, so he reached over and gently gave her a kiss. In all the fifty-five years of their marriage he could never remember missing a night giving his wife a goodnight kiss. Even when they had been arguing.

There had been three woman that influenced his life, and he would always hold them dear to his heart. His grandmother, Hilda May, whom he named one of his daughters after, his mother, Clara, and his dear wife, Sylvia. The bed felt so comfortable; warm and cozy, and with the snap, crackling sound of the fireplace it wasn't long till he fell asleep.

Outside, the dark gray clouds were slowly gathering. Then, from way up north, Ol' Man Winter took in a deep breath and blew it out, sending an icy chill through the late night, all over Cracker's Bend. The leaves still left on the trees shivered, gave way, and fell to the ground. The wild critters felt it in their bones, and knew it was a warning for what was to come; winter is here so it's time to find shelter.

Their God-given, natural coats were growing long and shaggy; a barrier against the winter elements. For weeks now, the squirrels had been gathering grain and nuts, storing them away in old, hollowed-out trees. The birds that stayed the winter had been feeding from left-overs in freshly picked cornfields, and sitting in rows on telephone lines and around chimneys, warming themselves. The early mornings were cold with mists laying heavily over the fields and timbers.

Chapter 3

"A Time Of Need."

Morning came, and the inviting aroma of Sylvia's coffee woke Horace from a sound, restful sleep. Sitting up on the side of the bed, he finally located the house slipper that had scooted under his bed. Finding his nice, warm, wool robe he ventured down stairs to the scrumptious breakfast Sylvia was preparing. Smiling and giving his wife a quick peck on the cheek as he passed her, he opened the kitchen door to take in a breath of early morning, fresh country aroma. He was caught in a winter blast of frigid air. Now he knew for sure it was time to bring the winter coats, mittens, and sock hats out of moth ball storage.

"Horace, please shut the door!" Sylvia commanded. Horace, pretending not to hear her, stepped out on the porch to see the cattle gathering at the fence to feed. "Brrrr," he thought, watching the steam coming from their nostrils, as well as his own.

Sylvia stood turning the page on the calendar hanging on the wall next to the refrigerator. She commented, "Tomorrow is the last day of October! Halloween is already here! You'd better come in out of the cold, Horace! You don't want to catch a cold."

He shut the door behind him and sat down at the table. He gazed over at her and grinned to himself, for his heart was full of joy, and everything was perfect in his world today. He started reciting something taught to him many years ago, when he was a boy, while attending a one-room country schoolhouse, not far from here, called White Oak Grove. Horace was known to do that at times and it always got a chuckle out of Sylvia.

He recited from memory: "Goblins and ghosts, spirits and spooks, witches and broomsticks, pumpkins on stoops, dancing shadows, flickering light, giggling of children, lost in the night, beware of the trickster, the spell that he weaves, the full moon is watching, on All Hallows' Eve."

Sylvia laughed as Horace paused a moment, giving her a wink.

"Robert Frost has nothing on you, my love." Sylvia said, placing a platter of sausage and bacon in front of him, and bending over to give him a peck on the forehead.

Horace laughed, and commented gingerly as Sylvia sat down beside him. "I loved that poem, it always gets me in the spirit of celebration! Good thing I brought in the last of the pumpkins and squash yesterday. Those clouds overhead certainly look like snow. I think we are in for an early winter this year, Sylvia."

Sylvia sighed and continued eating slowly, reflecting on the many happy and lasting memories of winters in the past.

"Oh well, Horace, we have nothing better to do but put another log on the fire, sit together by our window, look out over the farm, and watch it snow."

Horace was silent, thinking back on times when he had more than plenty to do—feeding stock, mending fences, keeping the farm machinery in working order, preparing for another planting season. He could recall days throughout the winters he would have to go down to the pond, and saw a chunk of ice out so the farm animals could get a drink. Now his son, Luke, farmed the five thousand acres, using the finest machinery money could buy, even installing heaters in the water troughs. It was considered one of the largest grain farms around this area. Along with all that, Luke feeds a large herd of Black Angus cattle over at his place having the help of hired hands.

The phone rang, and Sylvia got up from the table to answer it.

"It's Sheriff Hauser." Sylvia reported while handing the phone to Horace. At times Horace had filled in for the local dispatcher down at the Sheriff's office and was well acquainted with the local lawman.

"Yeah, Clifford, what's going on?" Asked Horace questionably. He listened for a long time, and then Sylvia heard him say, "Well, Clifford, I'll have to talk it over with Sylvia first, then I'll get back with you."

He hung up and walked over to the old Ben Franklin heating stove and put a stick of wood on the fire. Outside, the snow was beginning to fall lightly. Pouring himself another cup of coffee, he rejoined his wife at the kitchen table.

Sylvia just figured the Sheriff wanted him to come in and help out in the office, so she was not prepared for what he was about to propose....

"Horace, what did Sheriff Clifford want?" She asked.

Horace began to tell his wife the story. "Well, Sylvia, Clifford just picked up some homeless kids. He found them eating out of garbage cans downtown."

Sylvia closed her eyes and shuddered, imagining the sight. "Oh, no! How old are they?"

"Clifford said they've been hiding out in the Stinson's old abandoned house. The oldest is J.C., and he is 15 or 16 years old.

He has been trying to take care of his two younger siblings, April, four years old, and Harry is five."

Sylvia listened, and then asked, "Where are their parents?"

Horace shrugged his shoulders, and replied, "I don't know, and Clifford doesn't know either. That is why he called, and is asking us if we would take them in until he finds out. He doesn't have any place to put them, except to lock them up in jail. Once Child and Family Services gets involved they more than likely will be separated and placed in foster care homes."

Horace was quiet for a moment, finishing up his meal, then said, "Clifford said they are pitiful-looking, and very frightened."

Suddenly, Sylvia stood up, urgency sounding in her voice, "Horace, let's get dressed right now, and go get those kids. They need us!"

Rushing over to the closet, she got out her coat, galoshes, scarf, and mittens, throwing them along with her purse on the couch, saying, "Come on. Hurry, Horace, we haven't a minute to lose!"

They hurried upstairs to dress. Then, still bundling up, they headed for the car parked in the garage. This was not unusual for them to take in stray children. On several occasions they had taken in a wayward child until they found them a good home. But this would be the first time of taking in three.

They drove the familiar country roads in silence as the gentle snow kept falling, covering the countryside. Soon they were pulling up in front of the Sheriff's office. After parking, Horace took Sylvia's arm, helping her over the slick sidewalk so she would not fall.

Sheriff Houser met them at the door, saying, "I sure hate to get you folks out on such a day, but I felt this was an emergency."

Helping Sylvia off with her coat, and hanging it up on the coat tree, he took them into his office. Closing the door behind him, he offered them a chair as he sat down behind his desk and started to explain the situation.

"Sylvia, Horace, I'm going to be up front with you. I thought I would know something before you got here, but these kids are very close-mouthed. They are not saying anything, and are very scared they will be separated. They remind me of a trapped critter that has been caught. J.C. is very protective of his brother and sister. I have no idea how they got here, where they came from, or where their parents are."

He was quiet for a moment, then gave out a sigh. Leaning back in his chair, feeling it had been a long night for him, he said, "I'm very amazed they stayed aloft all this time without someone spotting them before now. I guess they stayed hidden in the old Stinson house during the daylight, and came out after dark to find food. I've tried to talk them into letting Doc Bentley take a look at them but they wouldn't hear of it."

He looked over at horace and Sylvia, sitting there, silently taking it all in.

"Now Sylvia, Horace, I know how you have taken children in for us before, and gave them a place to live for a while, but I've got to be honest here, and say I have never seen a worse case of abandonment than this one. So, if you change your mind after seeing them, I'll understand."

Horace stayed quiet, but Sylvia spoke up as she rose to her feet, "Clifford, we have already discussed this matter. These children will be going home with us!"

They all walked into a small office room where they found the children sitting close together on a small couch. Their hearts went out to them immediately as they saw the dirty, ragged clothes they were wearing—not nearly satisfactory for this harsh weather. They were smelly from uncleanness, undernourished, and shivering from fright.

J.C. the oldest looked to be about 15 years old, maybe 5' 7 or so,125 pounds, light brown scraggly hair and the brightest blue eyes Sylvia had seen since her eldest, Luke, was born.

Harry, the other boy, couldn't have been older than 5, just as the sheriff had said. Of small build and height, he also had features much like his older brother.

The little girl, though, was different. She looked like an angel that had fallen from grace. The brightest red, tangled hair, and the same blue eyes that seemed to run in this particular family, April couldn't have weighed more than 35 pounds soaked and wet. Even sitting in a police station under the direst of circumstances didn't change the inner beauty that shone through her ragged clothing and dirt-stained, four year old face.

Sylvia moved slowly toward them, and they held onto each other as if afraid of anyone coming near. Sheriff Clifford introduced them and said, "Now kids, this is Sylvia and Horace Deterding, and they have graciously volunteered to let you live in their home till I locate your parents."

Sylvia extended her hand to them, softly saying, "Hello, children. We would be honored to have you come to our home, and be part of our family. If you agree to come with us today, I have a good, hot meal waiting, and nice, warm beds for you to sleep in. Please don't be afraid. We just want to help you. You will stay together, with us; you won't be separated, and God will watch over and protect us all."

As she talked, she was inching her way closer, and smiling. Offering her open hand to the little ones she could feel their uneasiness and fear. Little Harry moved closer to his big brother, saying nothing, as April hid her face, holding onto J.C. Then, suddenly, sobbing, she came running into Sylvia's arms.

Finally, J.C. spoke, "We appreciate your offer, and we will take you up on it, as long as we can stay together." Then he paused. "When I get a job I'll pay you back for taking us in."

This touched Horace and Sylvia's hearts so that tears formed in their eyes. J.C. stood straight and tall as if all he had to offer was his dignity, and his good word.

Horace put his arm around J.C.'s shoulder, saying, "Well, young man, that's good enough for me! Now, let's all go home."

They walked out into the now blizzard conditions to the car. Sylvia carried April in her arms while Horace picked up Harry. The children sat close together, shivering, as Horace put the heater on high to warm them up. Sylvia made a mental reminder—tomorrow we will go to town to buy coats, hats, galoshes, and mittens.

Chapter 4
"Welcome."

Parking in front of the house, they went in. Sylvia hung her coat up and put away her purse. She turned to the children and instructed them to follow her. She took them into the bedroom where she had found some clothing for them to wear that had belonged to her children when they were small.

"Now, J.C. and Harry, you go into our bathroom and take a good hot bath. One of you can use the shower and the other the bath tub. I will help April with her bath after you two get through. Here are clean clothes. I think these will fit you till we can buy you some better ones."

They stood there as if they had no idea what she was talking about.

Then it dawned on Sylvia, "These kids have been homeless all their lives, and don't even know what I'm talking about. But, surely, sometime they have taken a bath..."

She had them come in to the bathroom, and showed them how to turn on the faucets. She showed J.C. how to put his hand under the water to test the temperature. When it was just right, she filled the bath tub half full and put some bubble bath in it. That caught Harry's eye right off, and he practically jumped in—dirty clothes and all!

Closing the door behind her, Sylvia took April into the half-bath downstairs to wash her little face and hands, taking her dirty, ragged clothes.

Wrapping her in a big, soft, pink towel, Sylvia asked, "How does this feel?"

April smelled it, and snuggled right up in it, for it felt so warm and soft. "Pretty." She said.

Sylvia laughed, and said, "I have a pretty little blouse, and nice warm slacks for you to put on when it is your turn to take your bath. And look, here is a warm sweater that will just fit you fine!" Sylvia hugged her close and smiled.

"April is such a pretty name." Sylvia tried to start a conversation up with the little girl who was not so frightened now. April looked up at her bashful-like, just taking in what Sylvia had to say.

On the little girl's arm she noticed a mark. "Oh my, did you hurt yourself?" She asked.

The little girl shook her head "no."

Sylvia washed it gently and looked closely. Shocked, she realized it was cigarette burns! Not wanting to frighten the small child, she made no further mention of the horrid marks.

The boys came out washed clean and smelling like bubble bath. Sylvia sat them down and gave them some leftovers from breakfast. April grabbed a piece of sausage and devoured it as the boys dug in with their hands, starved. She poured them some milk, and took a glass in with her as she took April into the bathroom to draw her bath water. To her surprise, the boys had left their clean underwear untouched. This puzzled her but she would ask them later about this.

April had the best time in the bubble bath water, splashing around and giggling. Sylvia helped her dry off, dressed her, and they joined the boys in the kitchen.

As Sylvia washed up the dishes from their snack, and started preparing dinner, Horace took Harry and April with him to watch TV. J.C. was still eating. Sylvia watched him eat as she finished the dishes.

"J.C., I'm curious why you or Harry didn't put on the underwear I had laid out for you," asked Sylvia.

He looked at her as if he didn't have the slightest notion what she was talking about. That was when she found out the kids had never worn any, and did not know what they were for. Evidently their parents got their clothes wherever they could pick them up free. They were on the road constantly, and never knew a home. Tears formed as J.C. told her parts of their lives but was very cautious in telling her the names or whereabouts of their parents.

That night J.C., Harry and April found out what pajamas were for. Sylvia had them put the flannel coverings on and join her and Horace in the family room. The snow storm was getting fierce outside, but the newly formed family were toasty warm before the fireplace. And, probably for the first time in their lives the children were clean, warm, safe, and had their tummies full. Horace,sitting in his favorite recliner, picked up a book of rhyme and prose and asked if everyone would like to hear a short verse or two? Nodding their approval, the smaller ones sat on the floor and listened as J.C. moved to an easy chair. Sylvia took to her rocking chair and started mending holes in Horace's socks.

Chapter 5

"A Safe Haven."

"The Miracle Of A Snowflake"

It floats like a whisper, a feeling, a thought.
Swayed by the wind, it wants but for naught.
It glides without effort, a blink in the night.
It falls to the ground to vanish from sight.

Yet, though we can't see it alone on the ground,
We know it's not lost but has really been found.
For it's purpose is simple, it's beauty redone.
To unite with the others, and together make one.

"The first fallen snow brings miracles aplenty." Horace continued to read from the old tattered book of his childhood. "Little children playing, laughter heard outside my window is medication to my soul and joy to my heart. Snowball fights lead to a snowman being created from a "baby" called "Snowflake." Not one is alike, because God made them that way. Late at night, when everyone is sound asleep in our cozy warm cottage, visitors come to play on our front lawns, hillsides, and ponds. The wind stirs over crusty frozen terrain, picking up speed as it travels. "Snow Rollers," they're named, magically appear. Rolling around on the ground, they're having the best time, as if they had a mind and spirit of their own, forming snow balls of all sizes and shapes as they roll around on the ground in play."

"Snow Angels, in lacy snowflake gowns, are floating down from their icy palace on high. Gliding gently from the sky with fragile crystalized parachutes, landing on soft pillows of glistening, soft, white snow. The Snowman family on the front snowy lawn suddenly, mysteriously, miraculously comes to life, dancing with delight as the man in the moon smiles down, laughing his head off, enjoying the sight. The Milky Way galaxy brightly marks the black velvet night, as does the Big Dipper."

"And then, at midnight, the magic appears! It has come to life with the arrival of Mr. Winter's wonders. But, only children, puppy dogs, kitty cats, and those with gentle hearts and open minds can see these miracles."

The children were peaceful, Harry and April sitting Indian-style on the floor, J.C. starting to drift into slumber, as Horace finished reading and slowly closed the book. Sylvia led them to their bedrooms, tucked them in, and they all retired for the night.

Horace, putting his pajamas on, laid down on the bed, listening to the burning wood in their bedroom fireplace crackle and pop. His mind was full of the happenings of the day, wondering how anyone could abandon such sweet children. Inside the two-story, old farmhouse the children soundly slept, touched by "gold dust" sprinkled by none other than Mr. Sandman. Sylvia turned out the light and came to bed. She was worn out, but very satisfied they had done the right thing today.

The clock struck 1 a.m when Sylvia was awakened by the sound of a crying child. She got up realizing it was coming from April's room. She slipped in and found the child huddled in the corner of the dark room.

Rushing over, she took her in her arms.

"April Dear, what is the matter?", asked Sylvia pleadingly.

The little girl put her arms tightly around her neck sobbing, "There is a mean man in the closet!"

At that moment the light came on and there stood J.C. and Harry in the doorway. They also had been awakened to the sound of their sister's troubling event.

April went to her older brother, and J.C. picked her up in his arms.

As he held her, he explained, "It's okay April, no one will hurt you here. You're just having a nightmare." They had recently slept in alleys and doorways and it had been frightening to them all.

"But it seemed so real J.C. I'm scared!"

"Don't be scared, April. Just remember we're still all together, and God will watch over us, just like Mrs. D. told us."

"Okay J.C. I'll try." Whimpered April.

Sylvia and April walked with the boys back to their beds. After tucking them in, they returned to April's room. Sylvia found her daughter's old teddy bear, and helped April get back in bed. As she pulled the covers up around her, she gave her Mr. Jiggs to hold onto and love. Sylvia told her Mr. Jiggs wouldn't let anyone harm her, that he was there to protect her, too. Then, she sat down in a nearby chair until the child was asleep. Leaving a nightlight on and the door open between the bedrooms, she finally slipped off to her own bed.

Days turned into weeks, and nothing was discovered to lead them to the children's parents. Luke took J.C. under his wing and was teaching him the occupation of tilling the soil and operations of the farm. The children were adjusting smoothly into a daily routine. After thorough physical exams by Doc. Bentley Sylvia enrolled them in school. Even though they had hardly attended any school in the past, having been dragged from one place to another, they picked up on their studies fast with only a few setbacks that Sylvia managed to correct. She tutored the children along with their homework, and soon they were at the same level as their classmates.

One November afternoon, April jumped off the school bus, running into Sylvia's arms, crying. J.C. was angry, and Harry was trying to console his little sister. Some children had been making fun of her, calling her names. Sylvia took the kids into the kitchen, drying April's tear-filled eyes with the hem of her apron. She picked her up and sat her on her lap.

"What names have the other kids been calling you, April?" asked Sylvia.

"They said I didn't have no folks cause I was ugly!" Muttered April. "I don't ever wanna go back!" The two boys sat at the table, and said they didn't want to go back to school either.

"Don't listen to those who only want to hurt," said Sylvia. "You three children are beautiful, and the only ugliness was their words." They talked the problem out, and then lovingly, Sylvia told them that they were part of their family now, and no matter what the future would bring, or where they would be, they would always be part of their family.

Then she added sternly, "You tell them bullies that if this ever happens again, your adopted mother will come down there and have a serious talk with them—and they will not want that to happen!"

Sylvia had taught school before marrying Horace. She was a very good teacher, and could handle any situation, or difficult child brought to her, with a firm hand and a lot of hard love. These children had found a safe place after years of abuse and neglect.

Chapter 6

"Thanksgiving."

"Open hearths, fires built high, wood crackling, sizzling their sleepy-warm lullaby in cozy parlors. Chimneys smoking in gray narrow streams over rooftops in winterish skies. Turkey baking, glazed-over and stuffed with scrumptious dressing, and steaming hot giblet gravy. We gather around a feast table celebrating harvest time, a celebration honored through generations since the first Thanksgiving Day!" (from the book "Rhymes and Reasons, Changing Seasons.")

Thanksgiving day came, along with all the wonderful aromas of turkey, dressing, and all the trimmings coming from the kitchen. The family, Hilda, Tabitha, Luke and his wife, Margery, and their three children, Moreen and her husband, Jake, and their daughter, April, J. C., and Harry gathered around the festive table and the food was blessed. Everyone was having such a good time discussing an amazing family trip coming up soon. Then the phone rang. It was sheriff Hauser.

Horace was the one to answer and get the news. He motioned for Sylvia to meet him in the kitchen alone. The children's parents had been located, arrested in Texas for attempted armed robbery with a weapon and drug possession. They tried to flee and were both shot. They had been rushed to the nearest hospital but had eventually succumbed to their wounds.

Sylvia looked seriously at Horace and said, "Horace, don't tell the children today. Wait till tomorrow. This is the first real holiday they've ever had, so let them enjoy it. They probably had no idea where their parents were or what they were doing. To burden them with this news now would only do more harm than good."

"I don't like secrets, especially one this important," confided Horace, "but this time you're probably right. No good would come from ruining the first real family gathering the children have ever known."

So, they all finished their meal, and Sylvia and the women folk did up the dishes. Then they joined the men in the den, now sitting comfortably before a warm, cozy fireplace, discussing farming and the prices of corn. April was playing with Mr. Jiggs with her new found family as Harry and J.C. were sitting listening to Luke and the other men. Horace picked up a book and sat down in his big stuffed chair. He had read this old, worn out book to his children and grandchildren every Thanksgiving; a tradition they all looked forward to.

April came over with her teddy bear, and Horace lifted her up in his chair as he turned to the first page. Looking around at the smiling faces he thanked the good Lord for the blessings given to him and Sylvia. Then, before his story, he started reciting another old poem he could recite by heart at any given moment:

Children sleeping, dreaming dreams of happiness and glee.
Decorations of the season adorn the tall pine tree.
Sugar plums and candy canes, ice cream delight.
Christmas carols, ringing bells, laughter in the night.
Cheerful giving, helpful lending, graciousness abounds.
While a solitary figure slowly makes his rounds,
Filling stockings overflowing, then off into the sky.
I'm short, I'm fat, I'm full of love...who am I?

April raised up with a big smile and yelled, "Santa Claus!!" Everyone laughed. The children had never been visited by

Santa, for their parents were too involved with themselves to bother seeing their children had a nice Christmas.

"You're right, of course," Horace said, whispering low, "But, not all are asleep." Reaching for the old book of rhymes and prose, Horace began to read aloud.

April was taking it all in, lying there wide-eyed against his big shoulder as Horace continued: "Mr Field Mouse and his family are scurrying about downstairs in the kitchen, staying far away from the temptation of the cheese-bated mouse trap! They had moved in from the cold through a knothole they found in the pantry wall. Curled up on the window-seat in the parlor is the precarious, curious, independent, old "Junior Cat"! He watches contentedly, through a frosty window pane, at the activity going on outside, unaware of Mr. Field Mouse, his narrow green eyes are taking it all in. Sweeping his long, striped, butterscotch, tiger tail back and forth, he makes a growling sound deep down in his throat. But, no one notices.... except for Ol' Mr. Field Mouse who signals his family, "It's time to scurry back through the knothole before Junior discovers us!!"

"The huge buck deer moves cautiously outside on the snow-covered lawn looking for corn or left over bird seed. Holding his proud crown of antlers high, sniffing the air, he is protecting his heard of seven."

"The big, old, cedar tree's branches are now drooping, draped with snow."

"The "Squirrel" family had worked hard gathering walnuts and corn, and stored it all away in the old, hollow, oak tree in the front yard. As the snow fell, they, too, were curled up in warm, pine needle beds, fast asleep."

"The "Rabbit" family with cotton-white tails are curled up close to each other keeping warm in the base of the old, hollow, oak tree.

The front entrance to their cozy little rabbit house had it's own little door, painted red with a green doorknob."

"Wolves were baying at the moon, creeping around way down on Big Indian Creek. But we, the Deterdings, are cozy warm gathered before the old fireplace and everything is peaceful down on the farm."

Horace loved to put a personal touch to the stories and poems in the old book by adding the family name in just the right places. As he looked down at April, her eyelids were just about to close.

Horace chuckled, and said, "It looks like we've got one down with the count. Someone needs to take our little princess upstairs and lay her on the bed, for she has already begun her nap."

Sylvia suggested J.C. take her into the spare bedroom downstairs. He picked his baby sister up gently, took her into the bedroom, and laid her on the bed. Sylvia found a blanket and covered her, leaving Mr. Jiggs clutched tightly in her arms. Sylvia and some of the women folk took the children into the kitchen and sat them down around the kitchen table, poured each an icy-cold glass of milk, put out a platter of home-made chocolate chip, peanut butter, and pumpkin cookies for an afternoon snack, and then went about preparing for the smaller supper meal.

Their grown children and families amounted to many; a house full now. Some would stay over at Luke's house. They would be there Friday and Saturday, and then all will be leaving on Sunday, after church and a big meal at the house. Most had flown in from long distances, and had to be back to work Monday morning, as well as the children going back to school. But, for now the family tradition, so enjoyed each year, will go on, bringing them all closer together. This family has strong and tightly knit bonds, never to be broken, lasting forever.

Horace never thought he would see the day when he would travel back to the hinterland where his ancestors had originated. In the 1800's, they journeyed from a small village nestled against the Alps, sailing out across the seas on their dangerous adventure to settle in New America. He sat in his old stuffed chair by the fireplace listening to the sporadic chatter as the family gathered around eating leftovers, visiting, talking about the family-planned Christmas holiday soon to be coming up in Germany. One thing they had not thought about in all the excitement was the children, J.C., Harry, and April. He sat there thinking, "After hearing the news about the fate of their parents, what will happen to them now!?" After everyone left or went on to bed Sylvia and Horace sat alone in the den.

"Sylvia, I've been doing a lot of thinking." He began. "We can't just go off on this trip and leave these children with strangers, or, in the hands of Family Services!"

Sylvia looked over at him, and then stared into the flames of the crackling wood burning in the fireplace.

She thought, this sure puts a different perspective on our plans, but these children's safety and well-being must come first.

"Yeah," She answered. "Little Harry was asking me today if he would get to go, too. And, if he would see Santa Claus there." She patted her husband on his hand, and went on, "I know, Horace, you are getting very attached to these kids, and so am I. We have to take one thing at a time, though. Now, don't get yourself upset. Everything will work out—all in God's time. It is in His hands." She gave out a little sigh, then was silent.

"But Sylvia, when we tell them about their parents, I hope that won't set them back. They have been doing so well!"

Sylvia stood up purposely and answered, "Well, Horace, we

can't control the future. Just leave it in God's hands. He knows what is best. Come, let us go to bed. We will worry about that tomorrow."
So, they climbed the stairs together and retired for the night.

Chapter 7

"Bad News."

Early morning came, and Horace raised silently from the bed trying not to wake Sylvia. Going on downstairs, and turning the overhead light on in the kitchen, he thought he saw a mouse scurrying out of sight. He reached for a cup in the cupboard and plugged in the coffee pot. Old Junior Kitty Cat came strolling in, rubbing up against the leg of his pajamas, trying to get his attention and a possible treat.

"Meow." (Good morning, of course, in cat language) Swishing his long tail, he sat down and looked up at him, so Horace grinned and stooped down to pick him up in his arms, giving him a loving squeeze, stroking his silky butterscotch striped fur. Junior Kitty belonged to a neighbor who asked them to take care of him while they left for the holiday week.

"Old Boy, you're slacking on your job. I do believe we have been invaded by a mouse!" Horace said, opening a can of cat food and placing it down on the floor for him.

About that time, J. C. entered the kitchen, sleepy eyed and yawning.

"Couldn't you sleep either, J.C.?" Horace asked.

Getting a glass of milk from the frig, nodding his head, no, J.C. sat down beside Horace at the kitchen table. "No, Mr. D." (The children had lovingly named them Mr. and Mrs. D., short for Deterding.) "Luke is going to pick me up early to get the last of the corn out of the fields, last minute catching up before the weather changes. I'm anxious to get out there on the tractor. I like working for Luke, and I really like farming."

Sylvia came into the kitchen wearing her printed granny nightgown covered with a cotton robe. Rollers were still in her hair, and she had no makeup on yet.

She went over to the stove, put her old teapot on the burner to brew a cup of tea, asking, "You guys are sure up early. Couldn't you sleep?" Then, seeing Horace playing with the cat, she added, "You'd better wash your hands after handling that cat, Horace, or you will have cat hair and germs everywhere!"

Hearing that J.C. was expecting to go with Luke, Sylvia spoke up, "J.C., we will need you to stay home with us today. Something has come up that we need to discuss with you and the other children."

J.C.'s smile had turned to a look of concern and worry. He remembered when he was very small, being handed from one family member to another. He had never felt the security he needed, or acceptance, until now.

The tea pot went off causing Old Junior Kitty Cat to take off in a dead run out of the kitchen into hiding.

"But, Mrs. D., Luke is expecting me, counting on me to be there! He will be disappointed if I don't help him in the fields!"

Feeling a little bit anxious now, panic was beginning to settle in, not knowing what was about to take place. It had taken J.C. longer than the other children to feel secure enough to confide in anyone or show his feelings. He had lived in fear all his young life, and when Harry and April were born, he took the responsibility of caring for them on his young shoulders. He had never known, or been given the luxury of being a child. Now that he had experienced acceptance and love from this family, he wasn't sure what to do with it, but he knew he never wanted to lose it!

"Wait a moment, Son." Horace began, trying to be as gentle as he could. Then he told him about the phone call. There was no expression of grief or outburst from J.C. He just sat and listened to what Horace was saying. They noticed his eyes moisten, but he showed no other outward emotion.

"I'll go and tell Harry and April, myself," J.C. said simply.

He stood up and left the kitchen heading upstairs. He went into the bathroom and closed the door behind him. Sitting on the floor, he put his head in his hands and cried.

Old Junior Cat, hating for any door to be closed in the house, saw that the bathroom door was closed, so he reached up with his paw, stretched long and tall, and moved the door knob enough to crack the door open. Wandering on in, he found J.C. huddled up on the bathroom floor. J.C. felt the warm soft fur brush up against him, then Junior lay down beside him and start licking his hand. It seemed as if Junior knew he was grieving, and was there to comfort him in his sorrow. He stopped crying and stroked the huge old cat, listening to him purring. Then he took Junior in his lap, buried his head in his fur, and closed his eyes as the tears fell silently. How am I going to break the news to Harry and April? He thought. Now we truly are orphans. I know they didn't care about us, but they were still our parents.

Sylvia started to get up to follow J.C., but Horace reached out for her hand and shook his head no. No words would console J.C. now. This step of growing up he would have to do on his own. They sat and talked quietly for a while, then went and showered. A new day, a new beginning for the kids, as uncertain as that was.

After breakfast J.C. took Harry and April into the den and told them about their parents. This time when Sylvia heard cries she rushed in with Horace following her. As soon as the young ones saw Sylvia, they came running to her, holding onto her tightly, sobbing. She held them tightly to her, telling them to not worry—she and Horace were there for them.

J.C. walked over to the window with his back to them so they would not see the tears flowing down his face. Horace stepped up behind him, placing his big hand on the boy's shoulder.

"J.C., we are here for you kids. We are not going to abandon you, Harry, and April. You're family now. And, we take care of, and look after our family."

J.C. turned and buried his head in Horace's chest, sobbing. He cried harder than Horace had ever seen anyone cry. Tears came to his eyes as he stroked the boy's hair, and he held him tightly. Horace didn't say anymore, for he too was choking up with tears. Looking over at Sylvia, their eyes met, and without words they knew what had to be done. A trip into town would have to be made. A trip that would forever change their lives, and maybe, just maybe, bring closure to J.C., Harry, and April.

Chapter 8

"Unforeseen!"

Several days later, after the shock had wore off some, J.C., Harry, April and Sylvia all rode with Horace down to the Sheriff's office. Now they would begin the process of necessary legal work. Horace and Sylvia wanted the children with them as they discussed the legal matters, (first with the sheriff, and then with whomever else it would take) to make this instant family legal in the State's eyes. Though the two smaller ones wouldn't have any idea what was going on, J.C. was old enough to understand. The most important thing to Sylvia and Horace was that the children would not feel like orphans. They wanted them to feel secure in the knowledge they were loved and wanted. No legal document in the world could accomplish that, but the close feeling, being together as a family while they all went through the necessary steps, would certainly help.

The children sat out front in the waiting room as Horace and Sylvia followed Sheriff Clifford into his office. Clifford wanted to know if the children had been told, then he proceeded to inform them that a family member had put in a request to the judge to take the two small children, but not J.C.

At first Horace and Sylvia sat stunned. Where had this come from!? As far as anybody knew, there were no immediate family members.

Finally gaining enough strength to speak, Sylvia protested, and confronted the Sheriff, "Where were they all this time when these children were growing up and needed them!?"

"What gives them the right to pick and choose who they want and who they don't!? Demanded Horace.

The Sheriff shrugged his shoulders. He didn't know any of the answers to the questions they asked. "Folks, I don't even know who these people are! What I have been told is they are from out of state."

That inflamed the Deterdings even more, that the kids would be taken far away so they wouldn't be able to see them again.

Sylvia sat back in her seat, and her face was flushed with anger.

"You're telling us, Sheriff, that the authorities would just hand over those little ones to strangers!? Separating them from their big brother who has looked after them, caring for them all their lives?!"

Sheriff Clifford looked over at her, knowing how much they had become attached to those kids. He remembered the three dirty, scared faces. He remembered the filthy rags that only vaguely resembled clothes. They had been through so much and just when hope was finally on the horizon....this happens.

He was silent for a moment, then replied, "I'm on your side, Sylvia," He said, trying to calm her fears, "But my hands are tied! I have to go along with whatever the Judge decides!" Shaking his head in disgust, he went on, "But, I have to warn you, ninety-nine percent of the time he decides in favor of the family."

Horace hadn't said much, but he stood to his feet, and in a firm voice said, "Well, Clifford, we are their family now, and we are going to fight this! I'm going to talk to my lawyer and see what can be done! No way them kids are leaving our house without a darn good tussle!"

Chapter 9

"On The Run."

The Sheriff shook their hands and wished them luck. He opened the door and they all stood in shock! The children were nowhere in sight! They had been listening at the door, and, apparently, afraid they would be separated, they silently fled....

Deputy Barns walked in, and the Sheriff asked him, "Where did the kids go?"

He looked around, lost for words, and not seeing them, he answered, "I don't know, Sheriff! They were sitting here huddled together when I left for about ten minutes or so."

Sylvia started crying, "Horace, we've got to find them! The weather is getting terrible outside. They must've heard us talking, and ran off!"

Horace put his arms around her shoulders, comforting her. Sheriff Clifford told deputy Barns to radio every car in the area, also, the State Police, and give them all the kids' descriptions, then put up road blocks in and out of town.

Sheriff Clifford came over to Sylvia and Horace assuring them they wouldn't quit searching till they were found. He suggested they go on home and wait. Horace and Sylvia hesitated, started to protest, then knowing they had run out of options, reluctantly got into their car and headed on home.

The snow was really coming down, almost zero visibility now. This certainly was a "Canadian clipper" coming down and looked like it would be continuing all night. Sylvia wiped her eyes with her handkerchief, and softly said, "Oh, Horace, they've got to find those children. April and Harry are so small. They can't survive out there in this weather."

Horace reminded her that they had dressed them warmly that morning in their new coats, boots, hats, and gloves.

"Also, Luke just paid J.C. yesterday, so he has some money to eat on." Horace said, trying to make Sylvia feel better.

That night there was no sleeping for any of them. The winter storm raged on, blowing fiercely around the northwest corner of the house, giving warning that this was no night for anyone to be outside. The temperature plunged way below zero, and the wind sounded sorrowful, like something hurting and in pain.

Come morning, the sun was out, but eight inches of sparkling snow covered everything. All the roads were blocked; everything was now at a standstill.

Sylvia called the family and told them what had happened. Hilda, their daughter in Philadelphia, married to a lawyer with two kids of their own said, "Mom, if we can help in any way, just tell us!"

Luke, married to Margery, blessed with three girls, knowing what the children had become to his parents, was heartsick when he heard the news.

If they'd thought the night was long, this next day was even longer. The roads were closed until the snow plow could get through to dig everyone out. All they could do now was sit and wait for the Sheriff's call. Sylvia's eyes were red from crying, thinking about the children being out in this dreadful weather; not knowing if they were okay, or what was worse, wondering what was happening to them. They could have gotten caught out in this frigid cold, and frozen to death. Or, worse yet, someone could've snatched them up as they were hitch-hiking; someone who would do great harm to them....

Horace sat in his old comfortable chair by the fireplace, and did a lot of serious thinking, along with praying, under his breath. The day wore on into night again, and nothing.....

Some calls trickled into the Sheriff's office of supposed sightings, but when the Deputy drove to investigate, they proved to be false calls or someone else looking similar to the children.

Another day passed, and by now the Sheriff was very worried. Although he did not alarm Sylvia or Horace, he thought they had been kidnapped; taken by force.

Luke and some local farmers had walked every inch of ground around there, but found nothing. Luke walked into the Sheriff's office with more volunteers on Saturday morning. They would search the frozen streams, rivers, timbers, and along the back untraveled roads. Another clipper was due that evening, coming down from the north.

Sheriff shook his head, and said, "Luke, I'm really worried. We should have found the kids by now. If we don't find them soon, I'm afraid we may never find them!"

Luke sat there, not saying anything, but doing a lot of thinking. After what must have seemed like hours, he asked, "Sheriff, you don't think they went back again to that old abandoned house they were living in before, do you?"

Sheriff Clifford looked stunned. He had not given it a thought. There couldn't be the remotest possibility...or could there.

"Luke, we boarded that up and nailed the doors shut," The sheriff replied slowly. "I…I don't think ..well, they couldn't have gotten back in there." He shook his head thinking about it. "I really don't know how they could. There is no heat or even a stove to burn wood in. The floors aren't safe to walk on; rotted out from age and weather. It would be far too dangerous."

They both sat there looking at each other. Then the Sheriff stood up and reached for his coat and hat. As he checked his gun, Luke said, "I'm going with you!"

Darkness had fallen early, and by the time they reached the snowed-in lane going back to the abandoned house, it was pitch black outside. The 4-wheel drive truck had a hard time making it through the deep snow. For over a half mile they plowed through the seemingly endless drifts, breaking a track until they pulled up in front of the dark, abandoned house.

The Sheriff turned his spotlight on, and slowly moved it across the front of the old abandoned farm house. The windows were still boarded up, but he noticed one had the boards off, could someone or something have pried them off?

"Sheriff, I think I saw something move." Luke whispered. They got out, and the Sheriff unlatched his gun holster just in case a pack of wolves were hiding in there. Sheriff called out their names…

"J.C., Harry, April! If you're in there, come out so we can see you! It is too cold to be staying out here. Now, come on out!" Nothing stirred…

Luke then stood in the light so they could see him.

"J.C., I know you kids are in there, and I know you are afraid. But, I swear I will not let anyone separate you from each other! I promise you! Now, come on out!"

Only the sound of the wind and the dancing of the shadows broke the silence. No movement from the house. Maybe the sheriff was right, thought Luke. No one could live in this place. Suddenly he picked up a small movement from the corner of his eye. It looked like...could it really be...?

April came running out into his arms, followed by Harry. Tears rolled down Luke's rugged face when he saw them. Picking them up in his arms, and holding them tightly, he said in a whisper, "Thank God, you're alive!"

Then, noticing a conspicuous absence, Luke asked them, "Where is your brother? Where is J.C.?"

April pointed to the old house, and there on the rotted down old porch, looking weather beaten but proud, stood J.C. Luke put the kids down on the ground, and went running, grabbing J.C. into his arms.

"Son, what were you thinking!? Don't you know how worried we all have been? We've been searching everywhere!"

J.C. started sobbing till his body shook as Luke held him.

"Son, you don't have to carry this tremendous load of responsibility on your young shoulders alone, anymore. You've got me, and Dad, and Mom to lean on now. We are going to help you kids through this! And, as God is my witness, we are going to do everything in our power to keep you kids together. I don't know how you managed to survive out here alone in the cold and without food. Maybe it was our prayers, maybe your strength and fortitude. However you did it, we all thank God you did. Come home with us now—your home."

The clock struck 11 p.m. The snow was still falling heavily when Horace and Sylvia noticed the Sheriff's vehicle drive in the driveway and shut off it's lights. Sylvia turned on the pole light outside as the porch lights came on. When they saw the children stepping out they were profoundly relieved. They all came into the kitchen and there was much hugging and crying. Horace thanked the Sheriff, but he told them to thank Luke, for if it hadn't been for him, they wouldn't have been found.

Luke held J.C. in his arms and looked him in the face, saying, "J.C., you remember what I said." He smiled down on him, and went on, "Besides, I need you to help me farm!"

J.C. nodded, and tried to get out a smile, but tears were still flowing down his face. Now he felt guilty for taking his small siblings out on such a wild journey in such terrible winter weather. He realized now he had put them all in danger.

Sylvia was holding onto April and Harry, looking them over to see they were not injured or frostbitten.

"Mrs. D., have you got something good to eat?" Harry asked, standing there in his bib overalls and sweater. She had to laugh and bent down and hugged him tightly.

"You bet, I've got something to eat! You go in, and take your sister, and wash your hands and face real good, and I'll have something ready by then."

Spotting J.C., her heart melted. Going over to him she heard a slight whimper and a sob. He whispered, "I'm sorry, Mrs. D." She took him in her arms, and Horace moved to her side putting his hand on the boy's shoulder.

Horace said, "Don't be so hard on yourself, J.C. You thought you were doing right, protecting Harry and April again." Sylvia held him and whispered, "J.C., we love you kids so much. Just like you are our own." He hugged her tightly and sobbed.

Luke followed the Sheriff out on the porch. Sheriff Clifford saw the tears in Luke's eyes, and said, "Luke, I'll do what I can."

Luke wiped his eyes with the back of his gloved hand, and said, "Sheriff, we are not going to stop till those kids are ours for keeps. It would break my folks' hearts if they were taken away."

Horace came out and said goodbye while the Sheriff took

Luke back into town to get his truck. As Luke walked to the Sheriff's vehicle he turned back and smiled.

"It's been a good night! I'll call you and Mom in the morning, Dad. You all get a good night's sleep, now!"

Horace waved back, calling, "We will now, Son! Thanks, Sheriff."

He stood for a while holding onto the porch post, supporting himself and watched them drive on out of sight. He said a little prayer, thanking God, with his head bowed in reverence. "Thank you, Lord. You came through for us again, and we appreciate it." Turning, he went back into the nice, warm, kitchen."

The kids were devouring big bowls of soup, with toasted cheese sandwiches and milk, as Sylvia was telling them, "You kids are going to take a nice hot bath, put your pajamas on, get under those covers, and get some much needed rest." She looked up at Horace and smiled. "We will all get some much needed rest tonight!"

Sleep, oh sleep, my precious ones, let none disturb your dreams.

May all your hopes and all your prayers be carried on moonbeams.

For beneath a blackened sky goes forth God's evening light,

Removing clouds of darkness, protecting through the night.

A beacon of angel dust to keep all safe from harm,

To lead the lost from trouble into His loving arms.

(From the book, "Rhymes and Reasons, Changing Seasons.")

Chapter 10

"The Hearing."

The Deterding family gathered at the courthouse; Horace, Sylvia, Luke, and Margery. Also, Hilda and Moreen had flown in to give their support. They sat together facing Jennifer and Lawrence C. Ballard. They were from a small town in southern Arkansas. Jennifer was the children's aunt on their mother's side. They had never met her because their parents had never stayed in one place very long, nor did they keep in touch with any family members.

The children sat outside in the hallway with Moreen until they were called in. Horace and Sylvia had hired a lawyer to appear before the judge representing them. Everyone in town was here showing their support, knowing the Deterding family, and how much they loved these children.

The courtroom was filled to capacity as the Ballard's lawyer came in and sat down at the table beside his clients. Horace and Sylvia gazed over at them, and they looked away. The court was called to order, and everyone stood for the judge to come in and be seated. They were to be the first case heard today, and were anxious to get it in session. The Ballards were sworn in, then proceeded to tell their story of why they wanted to adopt April and Harry. The judge listened as they told him they were unable to have their own children. They would offer them a good home, but didn't feel they could afford to take all three.

It seemed to drag on for most of the morning, while the children waiting outside the courtroom in the hall, were getting tired and anxious. Finally, the three orphans were called into the courtroom. Harry was the first to testify. He walked up to the front and stood very still and somber as he was being sworn to tell the absolute truth. April and J.C. took a seat between Horace and Sylvia.

The judge smiled down at Harry, so small his feet couldn't even touch the floor.

"That's a fine looking suit you're wearing, Harry. Is it new?" The Judge questioned.

Harry gave the Judge a great big smile and nodded his head yes. Pointing over at Sylvia, he said, "Mrs. D. and I went shopping, and she bought it for me, specially for today." He hesitated as he heard giggling through the crowd, then continued, "April got a new dress, and we both got new shoes, and underwear, too."

Everyone laughed out loud, and the Judge smiled and hit the gavel, "OK, now. Order in the court! Well, Harry, are you happy living with Horace and Sylvia Deterding?" He asked.

Harry's eyes lit up as he answered, "You mean Mr. and Mrs. D.?"

The judge smiled again and replied, "Yes, Mr and Mrs D. Do they treat you right? Do they treat you, your little sister, and big brother okay?"

Harry crossed his heart with his small finger and answered, "Oh, yes, Mr. Judge. They love me and April, and J.C., too. And we love them back!"

Tears welled up in Horace's eyes as Sylvia blew her nose and wiped a tear with her hanky.

The judge continued, "Would you like living with them for good?"

Harry's face lit up, and he clapped his hands, looking over to his brother and sister, saying, "Could we, Judge!?"

The judge probed some more, "Have you ever met Mr. and Mrs. Ballard, Harry? They are your Uncle and Aunt."

Harry gazed over at them and shook his head no, that he had never met them before.

Then the Judge said, "Harry, the Ballards want to adopt you and April. What do you think about that?"

Harry stood up and screamed "NO!" He then darted from the chair, running, grabbing Sylvia, burying his head in her lap, sobbing.

The Ballard's lawyer called April up to the stand. When he asked April the same question, she flat out yelled, "No!"

You could hear murmuring among the observers. When the the Judge asked her about her parents, she scooted way back in her chair, frowning, and was very quiet. When the Ballard's lawyer asked her questions, she refused to answer them. Then, the lawyer for the Deterdings stepped up. April recognized him as he smiled and shook hands with her, and she relaxed.

"April, could you tell us how life was for you and Harry and your brother, J.C., when you lived with your parents?"

April looked over at J.C., and he nodded his head yes, as if to say "go ahead and tell them."

"Well...Well...they were gone, and left us alone a lot. Sometimes we slept in the car. We didn't have a house like Mr. and Mrs. D. We would run off, but they would find us..."

Then she stopped, looking over at J.C and Harry. Harry moved closer into Sylvia and she put her arms around him. J.C. sat quietly, not making a move, nor did his expression change. The Judge asked April to continue.

"Well, then Harry would get a whipping, and sometimes they would make me go into a dark old closet. I cried to get out, but it was locked. Then Dad would beat J.C. when he tried to get me out." Tears were rolling down her small face and she whispered, "I was really afraid."

The Judge was having a hard time holding back tears himself, but he had her continue.

"Well, they would leave us, and not come back for a long time. We were hungry, and cold, and we...." She stopped talking, then, looking over at Sylvia and Horace, said, "Well, we would get food out of people's garbage cans sometimes."

There was a hush over the courtroom. So quiet you could have heard a pin drop. The Judge looked down on the small child sitting there so composed, and said, "Thank you, April. You can go back to your seat now."

The Ballards were silent, but you could tell the little girl's testimony had shook them to the core.

Next, Luke took the stand. Tall, muscular, and very handsome, he walked straight and proud to be sworn in.

The Judge questioned him about J.C. "I understand that J.C. helps you with some of the farming and chores around your farm, Mr. Deterding?"

Luke looked over at the Judge, and answered, "That's right, Sir."

The Judge asked, "Does J.C. seem to be a good worker? Does he cause you or anyone else any trouble?"

Luke spoke loudly, for everyone to hear, "J.C. is a fine, decent boy! A very hard worker. Being in the environment he and his brother, Harry, and sister, April, had to endure, I don't think anyone sitting in this courtroom today would have come out with the attitude this boy has. He could be a trouble maker with serious issues, and I wouldn't blame him if he was! But this is a boy who took big responsibilities on his shoulders that some grown men won't take on! I would feel privileged to call him my son!"

J.C sat silently, with tears streaming down his face.

Luke looked over at him, and then to the Ballards, continuing, "This boy….no, I retract that statement! This **young man** took care of his siblings when he was just a boy himself, and looked after them the best way he could. Finally, when the situation with his parents became unbearable, he took them, and ran off to find a better life for them all. Found and dragged back, he was beaten to a pulp. These children, Judge, were abandoned along the side of the road, with no food, no place to stay, and ragged clothes, not even fit to be wearing. The first and only real home they have ever known is when they came to live with my parents."

He was quiet for a moment, then continued, "Judge, it would be a crime to take these children, and split them up." He looked over at the Ballards. "Now, I don't know the Ballard family. They probably are good people, and I commend them for offering a home for April and Harry. But I do know my parents, and there is no better home in the world than the home I grew up in. They…we love those kids, and they are part of us now. And, it would be inexcusable to separate them after all they have been through; to take them from a family they have bonded with, and the people who have their best interest at heart!"

The courtroom burst out in applause. Everyone was clapping, with whistles and shouts of cheering as everyone came to their feet.

The judge waited, saying nothing, then said, "I'm going to take all this into consideration, and then give you an answer. Court is adjourned!"

Horace stood to his feet and asked, "Judge, if I may, I'd like to take a few minutes to ask for something more. We have had plans for over a year now, and are looking forward to a family vacation. The whole family is gathering, flying to our ancestral home in Oberammergau, Germany, to experience our origins. We plead with you to allow these children to come with us, to be part of our family. It would be such a wonderful experience for them, and we would love having them along. Is there any reason they can't go with us!?"

The judge looked down at Horace, and then at the children. Sylvia had her fingers crossed under the table. "You can take them with you, but make sure they are back here in this court room on January second, at 8:00 am!!"

Sylvia, Horace, the kids, and the whole family jumped to their feet, cheering the Judge, and hugging each other.

"Order in the court!" The Judge shouted out, but on his face was a slight grin. "Court adjourned, for the second time!"

Chapter 11

"The Trip."

December came, along with more snow! Sylvia was busy as a swarm of bees making honey in a honeycomb. She wanted to make this the best Christmas the kids ever had, considering they had not had any to speak of. She purchased all the gifts and hid them away in a safe place. Some of the small ones she would take with them to open on Christmas Day in Oberammergau. Horace, Luke, and J.C. chopped down a tree in the timber, hauled it in, and set it up in the foyer for everyone to see it when they entered their home. Sylvia would purchase a smaller, artificial one and decorate it for the den.

One night they gathered around with hot chocolate and homemade Christmas cookies to decorate the trees. They sang Christmas carols as they placed ornaments and tinsel on the big, old, fir tree. They would enjoy it until they left. The neighbors and Luke's hired hands would see that it was watered, as well as take care of the chores and watch after the farms while they were away.

Luke went out to the barn and hitched his big Belgium team up to a sleigh, and took turns giving the kids rides, and Grandma and Grandpa Deterding, too. The horses trotted along as the sleigh bells rang out in the chilly crisp air. A light snow was falling and everyone's spirits were high, anticipating the wonderful Christmas holiday yet to come. April and Harry scooted up close to Sylvia and Horace as they snuggled under the warm, old, wool horse blanket. There was much fun had by everyone. Sylvia cooked up a big dinner that evening, and they all sat around the table and visited, telling about times passed. Then, taking their hot drinks into the den, they settled around the fireplace and discussed Oberammergau.

The Saturday before they were to leave, Sylvia got Harry and April ready and took them into town to see Santa Claus. They were so excited, they began telling Santa what they wanted at the same time. Sylvia stopped them, reminding them to slow down and take turns.

Christmas was her favorite time of the year. It brought joy into the house, and smiles on strangers' faces as they went about preparing for the great event. Margery came over and helped Sylvia wrap all the gifts. Sylvia had asked the neighbors to place them around the tree just before they returned from their trip, so the little ones could believe Santa had left them while they were gone.

They all went over to the church and helped with the hanging of the greens. Sylvia introduced the children and promised that if they were able to adopt them she would see they were baptized there.

Finally the morning came to leave. Horace had slept like a baby, unlike Sylvia, who seldom could sleep before exciting events. Her mind would not shut off, thinking about all the things having to be done before they left. She double checked—medication for her and Horace, enough clothes for all of them for that whole time period, passports, money, traveler's checks, small first-aide kit, etc., and etc.

They were all to meet at Chicago's O'Hare airport to travel to Germany—back to the place this family all began; the Deterding roots. They were in such hopes everyone would get to go on this special family reunion. They were to meet at 10 am this morning. Luke would be bringing his van and Horace would be driving his truck carrying all the luggage under the hard cover on the truck bed, protecting it from the weather.

Sylvia raised silently from the bed trying not to wake Horace. She had seen to it everyone had packed their needs for ten days time. She looked at the clock, 3:00 a.m. She would allow them to sleep one more hour, then everyone would have to get up. Horace had already loaded the luggage that evening while she had placed out all the wool scarves, gloves, and all-weather coats to make sure they would be warm against the December biting cold outside. They would have 50 miles to drive to the nearest airport in Springfield, leave their truck and Luke's van, and all ten would board a shuttle plane to O'Hare in Chicago to meet with the rest of the family. She tiptoed down to the kitchen and turned on the overhead light. Making herself a cup of hot tea, she sat at the table and double checked her list (for the umteenth time)—making sure everything was done. She looked up, startled to see little April standing there with her teddy bear, Mr. Jiggs, clutched tightly in her arms.

"Child," she said, rising up to go to her. "Why are you up already?" Then picking April up and sitting her in her lap.

April whispered, "I don't want you to forget me, and leave me behind by myself."

Sylvia was startled, "Whatever made you think of that?"

She shrugged her tiny shoulders, "I don't know...it's just

sometimes...I remember waking up in the dark..all alone...and I get real scared."

Sylvia hugged her, saying, "April, we wouldn't go off and leave you, ever."

The little girl looked up into her face...and smiled.

After sharing a glass of milk and some hot cereal, they went back upstairs and dressed.

Getting Horace up took little effort as he was already awake and looking forward to the day excitedly. Sylvia then went into the boys' room. They were sleepy, but anxious and excited to get going on this wonderful vacation also.

Horace bundled up against the weather, got the truck out, and turned on the heater. J.C. and Harry would be traveling with him, while Sylvia and April would be going with Luke, Margery, and their daughters. It wasn't long till they saw headlights coming into the driveway. Sylvia lined them up, counting heads. Everyone present, she checked to see if everything was locked up and turned off. They were ready to go!

Horace knew these roads like the back of his hand. He could drive them blindfolded. His mind was flooded with many memories, so precious to him. He had farmed this very ground his great-grandfather, grandfather, and father had plowed. He'd made a fair living, was not rich by any means, yet not poor either. He would never trade the past hardships for all the riches in the world. Now he had the opportunity to walk on the very ground his ancestors walked so many, many years ago. Oberammergau would be their final destination before the end of this day...

He had read up on this far-away place, located in the picturesque Oberammergau Valley of West Germany's Ammer River. It is noted for their skilled wood carvers and the colorful frescoes decorating the walls of nearly every one of the town's low-roofed chalets, with whimsical scenes from well-known fairy tales and religious pictures of the Holy Family and the assumption of the Blessed Virgin, Mary.

Oberammergau is most famous for the Passion Play, telling of Christ's days on earth, from His birth to crucifixion and resurrection. This world-famous performance began in 1633. The bubonic plague was raging through Europe, killing off many. One hundred citizens of Oberammergau died then, and the elders vowed to reenact the Passion Play of Christ every ten years till the end of time if God would spare the town's remaining citizens. They kept their word, and so did God. From that hour, there were no more plague deaths in Oberammergau. The people of the little village have kept their promise, and this year marked another performance in the open theater.

Harry hadn't said a word, sitting close to Horace in his seat, bundled up cozy warm. J.C. was quiet, too, but he never was very talkative. It was noticeable to Horace that J.C. had something on his mind.

Finally, J.C. asked, "Mr. D., how does it feel to fly in an airplane. We've never been in one. Are they safe?" They had never been on a vacation like this, or any other, either.

"Oh, there is nothing to it, J.C.! It's like sitting in your chair back home, but you're thirty-four thousand feet up in the air!"

J.C. looked over at him. "Thirty-four thousand feet in the air! Isn't that kinda scary, Mr. D.!?"

Horace kept his eyes on the snow packed roads. "Naw, you don't even feel like your moving!"

Nothing was said for a moment, then he asked, "How many times have you been in an airplane, Mr. D.?"

Horace looked over at J.C., grinned, and said, "Never was, yet."

J.C. rolled his eyes and had to smile, then said, "That's not very funny, Mr D."

They turned in to the airport road and stopped in front of the terminal, letting everyone out and unloading the luggage to be checked in. Luke and Horace drove the vehicles to long-term parking and took a shuttle bus back to the terminal. After everyone was checked in and headed for their concourse, they found a cafe and had breakfast. April and Harry were wide awake now, very excited, taking everything in. Luke's daughter, Missy, and J.C. were the same age, and had formed a friendship, so they paired off together, found their gate and waited for the plane. Harry had his nose to the window, watching and counting every plane he saw land or take off. April sat in Horace's lap and leaned back on his chest. She thought he looked like Santa, in his bushy white beard. She was watching all the people as Horace was napping.

Finally their plane was ready, so they started boarding and finding their seats. Both April and Harry wanted a window seat, so Horace took Harry to sit with him while Sylvia took April to sit with her. J.C. let Missy sit by the window, saying something under his breath to the effects of, "If this thing goes down, I sure don't want to watch it!"

The small ones were completely fascinated, peering out the plane's small window. Horace was already missing the farm. He never was much on traveling, and this would be the first Christmas he would not be celebrating with the entire family in his own cozy, warm house.

The plane was crowded with people already traveling, getting an early start before the Holiday. The flight into Chicago didn't take long. Below them they saw train tracks, then, in the distance, huge buildings. Then, they heard the wheels touch down on the ground, and the sound of the air breaks.

J.C. grabbed Missy's hand tightly, and she giggled, saying, "J.C.! That's only the sound of the air-brakes! Everything is okay!"

The plane came to a stop, then taxied over to the unloading ramp. The family followed the rest of the passengers out into the lobby. Everyone had smiling faces, and all were talking at once. They had checked their luggage to go all the way into Oberammergau, so they wouldn't have to bother with heavy bags and suitcases. Standing around, glancing at his watch, Horace was watching the minutes tick away, getting a little anxious to board and get settled down in the jumbo jet's overseas travel. It would be a long trip, and he intended on getting some sleep before landing in Germany. He began to read the overhead monitor about their connecting flight from the concourse departure board. It was all running on schedule.

About that time, the rest of the family started gathering as their flights came in. Sylvia and Horace had gone to the post office weeks before and taken the children to get passports and their pictures taken. Now she put the documents safely in the inside pocket of her purse so not to lose them.

By the time their flight number was called, twenty of their family members were crowding around getting very anxious to board. April was jumping up and down, smiling and giggling.

Moreen picked her up in her arms, saying, "Well, Sweet Pea, how have you been?" It was very apparent the whole family had fallen in love with these children.

"Great!" shouted April excitedly. "I just rode an air..o..plane!"

"Well, let's get ready to ride an even bigger one." Moreen answered.

They all boarded the wide-bellied plane, and put their overnight bags in the overhead compartments. Sitting next to each other in their group, they took up a good bit of the plane. As they observed everything going on, April, Harry, and J.C. looked at each other and felt, for the first time, that they belonged in this big, wonderful family.

They landed in New York's JFK Airport for a short time to fill the fuel tanks and take on more boarders. Soon they were airborne once more, flying toward their destination. Everyone was so excited, anticipating the journey to the beautiful Bavarian Country that they had heard so much about from Horace. Luke was joking with J.C. and Missy, his daughter, and kept things light and jovial. They would be coming into Munich in the early morning hours.

Harry sat by Horace, his hero at the present time. He had never remembered having a grandfather, and Horace would be as close to a grandfather as he would ever have.

"Mr. D., have you ever been to Ober....Ober...ammer..gau before?" He asked.

Horace chuckled, smiled at Harry trying to get such a big name out of his small mouth, and answered, "No, Harry, this is my first time, too. I remember my grandpa speaking of it at times. The way he described it, it was quite beautiful, like a small village taken from a fairy tale story."

Harry laid up against Horace, resting from the long journey, and thinking about things that had happened to them since they came to live with Mr. and Mrs. D.

"Mr. D., tell me about Ober....Ober....ammer....gau. What will we see and do there? Will Santa Claus know I'm there?"

Horace pulled a pamphlet from his coat pocket and read some of the itinerary aloud.

"Well, lets see, Harry. It says here that Oberammergau is a small village, a magnet for tourism. Oberammergau is renowned for it's history and its wonderful selection of painted houses. And, oh, yes, Santa Claus knows where every little boy and girl is, at all times, all over the world."

Harry stopped him from finishing, asking, "What is a magnet, Mr. D.?"

Horace thought a while, then said, "Well, Harry, it is something, or some place, in this case, that draws people there.

They want to go there and experience it instead of just reading about it."

He continued reading out loud, "Most of the visitors arrive in the summer, drawn by the sights and the selection of the wood—carving and Christmas shops. In the winter they enjoy a variety of spectacular scenery and winter sports activities. Many people come for the cross-country skiing trails around the village. Germany has little better to offer in the winter than the treks out towards Linderhof Castle."

April and Sylvia was sitting next to them, listening intently. April's eyes got large and she leaned over and whispered to Harry, "We're going to see a real castle!"

"On a clear day," Horace went on, "With a magical beauty incomparable anywhere else with crisp snow and blue skies, people take in the winter sports. The village also offers a decent amount of skiing for the visitors, even if it is never going to rival the larger resorts to the south such as The Laber Mountain behind the town."

Harry clapped his hands, shouting, "Mountains! Can we climb a mountain, too, Mr. D.?!"

Sylvia chuckled, trying to visualize Horace, or her, climbing a mountain.

"Harry!" Horace said, "You are sure full of ideas this morning! We'll have to wait and see." Then smiled at him approvingly.

Harry didn't say anything for a while, just listened.

Horace continued, "The principal ski area is on the other side of the main road at the Kolben area, and offers a gentle selection of runs for beginners and intermediates."

Harry raised his head, and asked, "Mr. D., lets go skiing, or, at least, take a ride on those scooters that go on snow."

Horace smiled, and thought, "Oh, you mean a snowmobile?"

"Yeah, one of those."

April popped up her head and added, "Maybe we can ride it around the castle!!"

Horace laughed at their young enthusiasm to try new things. "Whoa, kids, I'm an old man! You will have to find someone younger to do that with. Maybe Luke will take you on one of those snowmobiles."

Harry shook his head and got quiet for a moment. "You're not very old, Mr. D." Harry said very seriously.

Horace put his hands through Harry's hair, smiled, and said, "Well, I'm too old to climb on one of them contraptions."

Sylvia asked Horace, "What does it say about visitors' accommodations in Oberammergau?" She was curious to know where they would stay.

Taking the pamphlet from him, she read it aloud, "Says here, lodging is plentiful due to the various attractions in the area—even if it is concentrated in the three stars and below class. It says Oberammergau is easily reached from the north and the rest of Germany via the motor-way south from Munich. The turn-off for Oberammergau is a short distance from the end of the motor-way. A good road from the south leads from Austria via Seefeld, Mittenwald, and Garmisch. A regular train service operates from the main Munich railway station. Most visitors would probably arrive through the Munich airport, further away than Innsbruck, but with mainly motor-way connections. Innsbruck airport is closer, but the roads are more liable to be closed in case of heavy snow. The roads to Salzburg is a more open route in the winter."

Horace listened, then said, "Well and good, but that is all Greek to me! I wouldn't know one road from another. I'll let Luke and some of the others figure all that out."

Some took a nap, read a book, and ate snacks. The time went

by slowly, but now they were nearing Munich. Soon they would be landing. Since it would still be dark, they would find a hotel to stay the night, then take the train to Oberammergau in the late morning.

Looking out the side passenger window, Luke was treated to the most spectacular sight he had witnessed in years. The blackness of the night disappeared to be replaced with a cascade of city lights. The scene reminded him of long nights he had spent on a tractor in the open fields, watching the stars dance in the heavens. Only this time the stars were dancing on the ground.

Slowly the plane descended as the beauty of the once darkened, now glowing, landscape came closer and closer. Tall buildings could be made out among the many shapes and sizes of the lighted structures that lay before his wide eyes.

"This must be how an angel would feel," Thought Luke. " To be able to survey God's creations and man's accomplishments from such an angle. What a rare and wonderful experience!"

As he pried his face away from the window and looked around, he noticed he wasn't the only one enjoying the sights. J.C. was also plastered up against the window, as was little Harry, even though he had to stretch over Horace's napping body. A long flight, but certainly well worth it!

Chapter 12

"Oberammergau."

The plane finally landed, they all got up, stretched, yawned sleepily, gathered their things, and slowly made their way out to the lobby. The hour was late, so not too many were around. They could see it was a large airport. Going down to luggage claim, they retrieved their luggage and now had to find a hotel that would take them all. This might be difficult.

"Dad, do you know how to drive here?" Luke questioned.

Horace laughed, "You kidding?"

Luke laughed, "Yeah, Dad, I am…"

Looking around they spotted an information desk nearby. They asked about hotels around the vicinity that could accommodate twenty people, the girl at the information desk started calling around to find rooms for them.

Sylvia commented, "I knew we should have made reservations before coming."

The girl hung up the phone and handed them directions to two nearby hotels with suites to handle all of them for the night. She suggested, in her broken English, that if any among them was not familiar with driving here, she could rent a long airport van that would carry them all around town till they caught the train to Oberammergau.

To their surprise, Moreen's husband, Jake, had been stationed in Germany while serving his time in the Army. So, he volunteered to be their driver, and everyone was so glad! They were tired and weary, and wanted nothing better than a good night's rest. The van was waiting, so they loaded their luggage, climbed in, and drove out.

The city was very large, streets well lighted, and very beautiful, even at night. They had no problems finding the hotels.

"Wow, Horace! Isn't Munich awesome!" Sylvia said, very impressed with what she was seeing so far.

Jake laughed, and said, "Mom, Dad, you haven't seen anything yet! Wait till the sun comes up, and you can see the city by daylight!" Jake drove up to the front entrance to let those staying there out. Missy said goodnight to J.C., for she was staying here with her parents, Luke and Margery, and her two siblings.

Jake drove on down to the other hotel, and let all the others out to check in for the night. He parked the van and walked into the lobby to register for their rooms.

The young blond girl bchind thc dcsk smilcd and spokc quitc fluent English, "Velcome to hotel Nymphenburg!" She exclaimed heartily, handing them their keys, and motioning for the bellboy to help with the luggage.

Jake asked her what was there to see and do in Munich?

"Are you going to be here for awhile?" She asked.

"No, we'll be heading out, either tomorrow or the next day, to Oberammergau." Jake replied.

She nodded her head in approval. "Oh, you won't be

disappointed with beautiful Oberammergau! The snows have started covering the mountain slopes, and the drive there is very pretty." She paused a moment, then went on, "Well, you might already know, Munich, Germany is the third largest city in the country, and one of Europe's most affluent cities. We are located in south eastern Germany, in the state of Bavaria."

She smiled and continued, "The city boasts an urban population of over a million. It is always bustling, both during the day and during the nightlife. A tourist in Munich will find no shortage of things to do and places to see. Much like Berlin, to the north." She handed them a pamphlet, and they went on to their suite to retire for the rest of the night.

The next suite over, Horace and Sylvia had put Harry and April into their beds while J.C. took the living room couch-bed. Then, Horace and Sylvia finally retired to their bedroom. Everyone went sound asleep as soon as their head hit their pillow.

They all slept in late that morning except for J.C. He was up early, dressed, and rode the elevator down to the lobby. He spotted the small coffee shop, walked in, and finding a stool up at the counter, he slowly sat down. J.C. had worked for his own money down on Luke's farm and was feeling quite grown up. He ordered a cup of coffee, black like Mr. Dee and Luke liked it, and an oversized jelly donut. He thought to himself, the girl waiting on him behind the counter was really cute, and she was certainly giving him the eye! He took a drink of the hot liquid. This was his first experience drinking coffee; Mrs. D. thought he was too young. He made a face, not expecting it to be so bitter. As he began loading it down with sugar, the young waitress smiled, and asked,

"You like some cream?" He nodded yes, thinking, "She's pretty, but right now my heart belongs to Missy, and no one else!"

"You're not from around here, are you?" She asked. J.C., always a bit shy shy, simply replied, "No. America."

He spotted a rack holding travel information pamphlets. Walking over he picked up a handful of them. He was surprised how many were in English. He finished off his doughnut, and started reading some of the pamphlets:

Munich's history is highly varied. It said. *It has been home to Holy Roman Emperors and a revival of gothic arts. Later, it was occupied by a King of Sweden, and suffered from the bubonic plague. Prior to World War I it was a popular home for artists and writers. Munich, Germany hosted the 1972 Olympics. The city has flourished in the good times, and persevered through the bad. Like most of Germany's cities, Munich has a rich amount of history just waiting to be explored in over a dozen museums within the city—including art, sculpture, photography, and technical innovations, just to name a few. A tourist's dream, there is much to see and do here. In Munich, you'll find many beautiful cathedrals such as the impressive Theatinerkirche. Munich is the home to the Bavarian Opera House, a classic theater with a reputation for phenomenal performances. Munich nightlife has all manner of activity located throughout the city. In the pubs you might see shelves with steins stored on them. They're kept there by the locals who want to drink out of their own whenever they visit their favorite place. Live music in the cafes offers both local and international sounds. Performing arts? You'll find plenty there as well. Whether you come to see the historic sights, or fantastic Oktoberfest (starting in September), or the nightlife, this city is full of pleasant surprises for any traveler. We have many American visitors. You will not want to miss King Ludwig 11's castle!"*

The late morning sun shone through Sylvia and Horace's bedroom window. She lay a moment, still feeling groggy from jet lag. She slowly rose up in bed, stretching her arms, thinking, a good cup of coffee would be great about now. Someone knocked on her door and she scrambled to find her robe. Opening the door she found a silver try with a rose, a pot of hot coffee, and two trays of food! Sylvia stood barefooted, looking around. Not a person did she see. How strange is this!? She thought. Maybe they have the wrong room...

She wheeled it into the room and closed the door behind her. Then she heard the phone ring and hurried to answer it. It was Hilda on the other end.

"Hi, Mom! Happy Anniversary! Did you get breakfast in bed this morning!? We all thought it would be nice for you and Dad to enjoy it together in your room. Our treat! Oh, there should be a separate cart brought up for the kids, too. When Jake is ready to check out maybe we can ride around the town to see it before leaving on the train for Oberammergau." She giggled, as only she could, because she had surprised them.

Having so much fun on the trip, Horace and Sylvia had almost forgotten it was their anniversary.

"Hello, Dad! Happy Anniversary, to you too!" Hilda called out, hearing her father in the background. Horace took the phone.

"Hi, Sweetie! I'm already eating my breakfast! Thank you!" He answered. "I was beginning to think your Mom had turned this into a Hardy Girls mystery, there for a moment. We didn't know where the free breakfast cart came from! Good thing you called. We wouldn't want to be eating someone else's breakfast!"

There was a knock on the door. Sylvia took the receiver from Horace, saying, "Hilda, someone's at the door. I think it might be the kids' breakfast cart. We will see you shortly. Thanks, Honey, for thinking of us."

Sylvia opened the bedroom door into the living room, and almost stumbled over April and Harry standing there, sleepy-eyed and hungry. She tipped the bell boy, bringing the cart in, then turned the TV on for the children. They sat down on the floor before the TV set, watching cartoons and eating. Sylvia noticed J.C. was not there, and asked about him. No one seemed to know anything.

"He was gone when we woke up." Commented April.

Sylvia went back into the bedroom and found Horace had finished eating and was taking a shower. Her food was cold, so she went back into the kitchenette adjoining the living room, and placed it in the micro-wave. Sitting down at the small kitchen table, she thought to herself, so much for breakfast in bed! The food she enjoyed. A warmed over, scrumptious breakfast alone, not so much.

While getting the kids bathed and dressed, she asked Horace, who was gathering up everything and packing it away, if he knew where J.C. went off to? He told her he would go down looking for him, and find out when Jake would be leaving. Horace rode down on the elevator and browsed through the lobby, picking up travel pamphlets, as he walked through, about places he thought might be interesting to visit. Looking over his shoulder, he spotted J.C. in the coffee shop. Jake walked in and put his hand on Horace's shoulder, they said a few words of greeting, and went on in to join J.C. over a cup of coffee.

Everyone was up and dressed, ready for a wonderful day of new adventures! Jake and J.C., loading the luggage, were surprised to find a new, light snow covering the ground. Harry and April came bouncing into the lobby, dressed warmly in cute ski outfits. Harry had chosen his, bright green, and April's was a blue that set off her beautiful eyes and long, silky, red hair perfectly.

Looking up at Horace, April said, "Ok, Mr. D., I'm ready to go!" Then Harry added, with great enthusiasm, "Me, too!"

Departing from the hotel, they all crowded into the van, and drove over to pick up the others. They all got settled in, and Jake drove out of the parking lot onto the busy street.

It seemed that everyone here drove at one speed—fast! They passed by the Munich Olympic Tower and then Munich Monuments: Olympic Tower. The information sign said: "If you are not afraid of heights, and want to see Munich from the highest point of view, welcome to the Olympic Tower! The view platform is a height of 190m. When the weather is clear you have a great view of Munich and it's surroundings. Sometimes you can see the top of the Alps."

Horace had read somewhere before that The Olympic Tower was built in 1968, with a height of 289.53 meters. Therefore, it is almost three times as high as the Wahrzeichen of Munich, and the Frauenkirche. In 2005, it received a new antenna and now it's height is 291.28 meters. Everything in Europe is measured by meters instead of feet. It provides TV and radio to about six million users in Munich and in the south of Bavaria.

He went on reading: "If you are hungry, or just want to relax and enjoy the view, there is also a restaurant on the Olympic Tower. The great thing about that restaurant is it revolves very slowly around the tower so you can enjoy the great view even more. The Tower has another attraction, the highest rock museum throughout the world."

Moreen called out, "Anyone for a rock museum!?" There was nothing but silence....

Then J.C. spoke up, "I don't think they mean rocks you'd find on the ground, but where you can view paraphernalia of famous rock stars like the Rolling Stones, Pink Floyd, and Frank Zappa."

The teenagers and young ones shouted and clapped to go see it, but Horace rolled his eyes, made a groaning sound, and made a circle with his finger, saying, "Whoopee! A rock star museum! Just what I always wanted to see! " He had to laugh when he caught some looks that conveyed "Old Fogey!" Then said, "I think we'd better start for Oberammergau. How far is it? I don't think anyone wants to get caught up in a blizzard."

"Dad! We can't go without seeing Munich's famous Nymphenburg Palace and Park, Amalienburg, Badenburg, Pagodenburg and Magdalenenklause (Hermitage) or Marstallmuseum (Museum of Carriages and Sleighs in the former Royal Stables). Oh! And also, the Munich Museum of Nymphenburg Porcelain. And, and...Cuvilliés Theater." Moreen was reading from a travel pamphlet she had picked up at the hotel. She was having a problem pronouncing the long german names.

"Moreen!" Sylvia stopped her from reading about anymore places. We won't have time to take all that in! Pick out one place, then after that we are heading for Oberammergau."

She gave a sigh, with, "Oh Mom! You're such a party pooper!"

Horace laughed, took Sylvia's hand in his, and said, "Well, Dear, you can join this old geezer even if you are an old party pooper. Where to next!"

They headed out for The Nymphenburg Palace. April was singing, "We are going to a castle, we are going to a castle!"

Harry shouted out, "April, will you shut up! You're giving me a headache!"

Everyone laughed, and April turned around in her seat and stuck her tongue out at her little brother. Sylvia gave her a warning look, shook her head no, and asked her to be nice.

Tabitha had not said much, but she loved observing the historical buildings and read about the stories behind them. "I see here, Dad, this castle was built as a summer residence for one of Bavaria's electors, Schloss Nymphenburg. Nymph's Palace, it's called. It says here, it is a treat for those who enjoy viewing the opulence of the lifestyles of the aristocracy."

Luke sat up front with Jake, watching the road and getting a first hand lesson on driving in Europe compared to driving in the USA. The Palace was located just west of Munich.

Tabitha continued reading, "The Nymphenburg Palace was commissioned in 1664, by Elector Ferdinand Maria, to celebrate the birth of his son, Maximilian Emanuel. The elector was to make this his summer residence and would live here with his consort, and the mother of his child, Henrietta Adelaide of Savoy. The architect chosen for the palace was Agostino Barelli, who designed the central section of the palace to resemble an Italian villa, much to the delight of Henrietta. However, the palace didn't maintain its original state for long. Five Wittelsbach rulers have changed or added to the palace." Tabitha read on, "Max Emanuel, the young man for whom the castle was built, was the first to make additions. And, in the year 1700, he added galleries and pavilions, extending the sides of the Nymphenburg Palace. Soon stables were added to the south and orangeries to the north. Further additions continued, especially throughout the 18th century. The facade was extended to an impressive width of 600m (1968 ft). It has these magnificent ceiling frescoes (paintings). After 1741, when Germany had allied with France and Spain against Austria, Nymphenburg Palace became the summer residence of the rulers of Bavaria."

Chapter 13

"The Castle."

The Ghost

I look in the mirror but see no reflection. I am lost..... I am lonely..... but I feel no pain.
Am I cursed, a solitary figure of hopelessness? To wander alone in this place in vain?
I feel no heat...I feel no cold...my senses are of light and dark.
My surroundings no longer luxurious be now simple, plain, and stark.
I must strive now to right this wrong, to cast aside the dastardly deed.
Turn away from selfish acts, help those who truly be in need.
Betrayal was my lot in life, contrition be my goal.
Relief for my longing spirit, salvation for my soul,
For this I pledge my essence of being, to fulfill my obligated part,
To know the warmth that comes from seeing, the purity of a loving heart.

About then, Jake drove into the huge estate grounds. They were awe-stricken at the beauty. Finding a parking spot, they all bundled up, got out, and stood gazing at the magnificence of the palace and beautiful snow covered surroundings. Walking up to the front of the huge building, the wind was blowing really chilly, so Horace put his arm around Sylvia to keep her warm. Jake was concerned that it would start snowing again, and wondered if his decision to drive, instead of trying to crowd everyone onto the train, had been such a good plan. He was not familiar with the roads to Oberammergau. Looking up at the sky full of snow clouds, he knew this would have to be a short visit.

They were beginning to climb the big hill to the castle when Hilda spotted a sign. "Oh, no! It's not open. Closed from October to March! What a bummer!" There weren't that many visitors that day at Nymphenburg Palace. Summer visitors were plentiful when you were able to enter, but most people in the winter would go to the Alps for skiing. They gathered together disappointedly, and walked back down to the van, snapping pictures of the lovely, fairy-tale castle sitting high on the bluff.

"The 19th-century old Knights German Bavarian palace sits on a rugged hill near Hohenschwangau and Füssen in southwest Bavaria, Germany. Although Ludwig did not allow visitors to his castle while he was alive, after his mysterious death in 1886, it was opened to the public to help defer Ludwig's mounting debt. It is now the most photographed building in Germany, and is one of the country's most popular tourist destinations. The castle has appeared in several movies, and was the inspiration for the Sleeping Beauty Castle at Disneyland Park. The palace is now owned by the state of Bavaria, unlike nearby Hohenschwangau Castle, which is owned by the head of the house of Wittelsbach, currently Franz, Duke of Bavaria. The location is very beautiful and unapproachable."

Moreen was reading from a travel pamphlet about the enormous, elaborate rooms that were decorated in their original Baroque style. Some, however, were redone in Rococo and Neoclassical style. Several rooms in the palace were even available for rent for special occasions.

"The stable of the palace houses a wonderful museum of ancient carriages and sleighs. Many were involved in historic events such as coronations," Moreen continued to read in the brochure, then commented, "Wish we could've stayed here a night. It sounds so romantic."

Disappointed, she put the pamphlet down, and quit reading.

Harry picked it up again and tried finishing the pamphlet's information and history of the castle and grounds. "You'll also find un..i..forms worn by guards and other serv…ser..vants, and a fine col…lec..tion of Nym..phe..n..burg (sounding out each syllable) por…por…I can't say that word!"

Disgustedly, Harry tossed the pamphlet aside.

J.C. and Missy slipped off on their own. She was acting like she was a princess of her castle, while J.C. was filming it with her camera phone. She was twirling around in the snow with the beautiful tall castle in the background, when she suddenly found she was alone! J.C was nowhere in sight!

She called out to him, "J.C. where are you? J.C.…J.C., quit playing games! Come out and show yourself!! If you don't appear in the next second, I'm going for my dad!"

Then, way up the hill, she saw him come out from behind the bushes and wave for her to come join him. She looked down toward the van. Everyone was milling around, taking pictures. She yelled down and said, "J.C and I are going on up and take pictures closer to the castle!" She saw her Dad wave and smile, so she turned and climbed on up further till she joined J.C.

"Look what I've found." He exclaimed. "It's a way into the castle, I think." They disappeared behind jagged rocks into a cave. J.C. and Missy cautiously felt their way. It was indeed a cave, with passages going off in all directions. The path they were on, though, was not that long, and a light seemed to illuminate their surroundings with a dim glow. They held on to each other, moving slowly, step by step, till they came to a huge open area out over the water. This was the source of the strange light. They were back out into the open, only it wasn't where they had started. There seemed to be a water-way leading out to a big area of water. A boat was docked, anchored there, and they wondered if someone was in the castle. They proceeded slowly, so not to be caught invading, listening for any sounds. Following the waterway, which they compared to the creek that ran by their farms at home, they found themselves in the open courtyard inside the castle grounds.

The palace is comprised of a gatehouse, a tower, the knight's house with a square tower, and a Palas, or citadel with two towers to the Western end.

J.C. and Missy, knowing they were in the open, needed to find a way inside before being discovered. They proceeded on, staying close to the stone wall, out of sight. Finally, they came upon a door, probably used now for deliveries, but once maybe, was an entrance to the servants' quarters. Finding it to be unlocked, slowly they slipped inside.

It was all so exciting as Missy started taking pictures. "Could we get arrested for being in here, J.C.?"

He smiled and whispered, "We'd have to get caught, first!"

He held her hand tightly, and they slowly continued deeper into the interior part of the old castle. Slowly they crept down the ancient hallway, keeping close to the walls.

"What mysteries must have taken place here. What tales of intrigue. If only these walls could talk," Thought J.C.

Missy continued taking pictures every chance she got, as together they purposely explored the old castle.

The suite of rooms within the palace contained the Throne Room, Ludwig's suite, the Singers' Hall, and the Grotto. Throughout, the design pays homage to the German legends of the Swan Knight. Hohenschwangau, where Ludwig spent much of his youth, had decorations of these sagas. These themes were taken up in the operas of Richard Wagner. Many rooms bore a border depicting the various operas written by Wagner, including a theater permanently featuring the set of one such play. Many of the interior rooms remain undecorated, and some features of the palace remained unbuilt. The foundation for the keep is visible in the upper courtyard. The finished rooms include the Throne Room, which feature a glass gem-encrusted chandelier, all Twelve Apostles and six canonized kings were painted on the wall that surrounds the pedestal for the throne—the actual throne was never finished, and Jesus, behind the pedestal. This reflects Ludwig's view of himself as king. The King's master suite includes a four-poster bed, hand carved of wood, the canopy of which is carved as the cathedral towers from every cathedral in Bavaria, a secret flushing toilet (which flushes with water collected from an aqueduct), and a running sink in the shape of a swan. The hand-carved wood is very detailed and adorns the entire room. This caused the master suite to take 10 years to complete. The palace also includes an oratory, accessible from the dressing room, and the master suite, which features an ivory crucifix, a room made to look like a cavern, a full kitchen equipped with hot and cold running water and heated cupboards, servants' quarters, a study, a dining room and the Singers' Hall. The Singers' Hall is a venue for performances by musicians and playwrights. The King built it for Wagner as a place to write and perform plays. Despite its medieval look, the construction of Neuschwanstein required the modern technology of the day, and the palace is a marvel of technological structural achievements. Steam engines, electricity, modern venting, a modern water system on all floors, and heating pipes is all part of the structure. Ludwig II was the first to bring modern inventions, and he pioneered the introduction of electricity into public life in Bavaria. His new palaces were the first buildings to use electricity.

Sylvia and Horace got back into the van, and Jake turned on the heat for them. The snow was getting heavier, and Jake was getting anxious to get back on the road. Margery joined them in the van, along with Moreen. The others were still filming and taking in the beautiful sights.

"I see the village of Hohenschwangau is near here." Moreen commented, then read from the pamphlet again, "It's a forty minute walk up the hill from Alpseestrasse to the castle. When it is open, the ticket center is in the village, along with a gift shop, guided tours, restaurants, and toilets. It says King Ludwig II grew up at Schloss Hohenschwangau, which is just a few hundred yards away from Neuschwanstein. Ludwig spent his youth dreaming of a past era of Medieval Knights and spending time alone exploring the surrounding Alps. His father was King Maximilian. He died suddenly, and then Ludwig became King of Bavaria at an early age. It says here he and the Bavarian politicians didn't get along because Ludwig spent so much money on these castles, especially this one they called "The Palace in The Sky." He chose to build on the ruins of Vorder and Hinterhohenschwangau, above Schloss Hohenschwangau, where he was raised."

As everyone drifted back toward the van, Hilda counted heads. She found two missing, J.C. and Missy!

Chapter 14

"Mysteries And Miracles."

Meanwhile, Missy and J.C. were having so much fun exploring the old castle they did not hear the men approaching. J.C. heard the footsteps first. He grabbed Missy, and shoved her into a closet-sized room, then he followed her and shut the door. Men's voices were heard outside in the corridor. They were speaking in German, and one seemed to have a French accent. But, one was plainly an American. His voice they could understand. They put their ears to the door and listened, trying to figure out who they were and what they were here for. They heard one say something about smuggling a priceless item out, and selling it for many euros (money) in America.

J.C whispered to Missy, "We've got to get out of here. They are thieves stealing artifacts." A priceless painting was mentioned, and the hair raised up on their necks. They knew they had to find their way back out and warn the authorities. They realized they were alone, within inches of dangerous smugglers, thieves that probably would think nothing about killing them if they discovered they were there.

"How can we get out of here when we don't even know where we are?" Missy whispered worriedly.

J.C. cracked the door just enough to see the three men packing a painting in straw, and nailing up another crate to be carried to the boat. He could also see they were packing pistols in shoulder holsters. One had a Bowie knife tucked in his belt.

The rest of the family had no idea what was going on up the cliff from them. They had gathered back at the van, unaware what trouble J.C. and Missy were into within the walls of the old castle. They all stood gazing over the surrounding area taking last minute photos of the park, canal, and palace.

"Where could those kids be?!" Sylvia said, worried now, getting out of the van, looking around to see if she could find them. She yelled out, "J.C...... MISSY!! Come on down now! We are leaving!" She saw nothing moving, nor heard any reply back. Darkness was approaching fast.

"We need to be heading toward Oberammergau before dark! I think it's like eighty miles from Munich, southwest of here." Jake commented, getting very anxious to get back on the road.

Luke whispered to Margery, "Something must be wrong! Missy wouldn't just disappear like this without telling us where she was going."

Margery leaned closer in to him, speaking low so that the others would not hear, "Luke, do you think they might be in trouble, maybe fallen off the cliff, and one is badly injured? Or both? Surely one would come to us for help if they were able to!"

Tears started trickling down her face as she asked, "You don't think someone could have kidnapped them?"

Luke put his arms around her to comfort her. "No. We must not think that way. The last thing Missy said was they were going up around the castle to take more pictures. Probably the time has just gotten away from them. It looks like quite a climb up there from here."

Now, doubt and fear were beginning to grip his soul. He suddenly had a sinking feeling, and he just knew those kids were in trouble.

"Margery, find your cell phone, and call her number. If they don't answer, call the nearest authorities and tell them we have an emergency up here. I'm going to take Jake, and Hilda's husband, Stu, and go on up the cliff to search for them before dark."

Margery found her phone, but could not get a call out. The mountains around the valley were blocking the signal.

"Anyone else have a phone here?!" She called out to the others, but they, too, could not find a signal. They would have to find higher, open ground. Horace and Sylvia came over to her.

"Do you think the kids are in trouble?" Sylvia asked, getting nervous; her voice shaking a bit.

The expression on Margery's face told it all, but she stayed calm and said, "I really don't know. Luke is gathering the men to go searching for them. Mom, Dad, don't worry. Luke is probably right about them having fun, and probably have lost all sense of time."

Horace walked over to the men. "I'm going, too!" He said defiantly, a little angry he was not included in the search.

Luke shook his head. "No Dad! All due respect, but we are younger, and I don't want to be worried that you will slip and fall. Besides, we don't even know what we are dealing with yet. You need to stay and and protect the women."

Although Horace didn't like being bossed around, he thought over what Luke said. He knew he certainly wasn't a spring chicken anymore, not agile like he use to be, so he reluctantly agreed to stay back with the woman. The three men started climbing up the steep hill toward the cliff and castle entrance.

J.C. closed the door silently so the men would not hear him and Missy trapped inside the small utility closet. He leaned in to her, whispering, "We will wait till they carry that big crate down to the boat, then we'll make a run for it."

She was trembling so he put his arms around her. "Don't worry, Missy. We will get out, and back down the mountain without them knowing..." About that time, Missy's cell phone rang in her camera case. Just once, but enough. She rushed to get it out and shut it off, but was too late.

The men stopped what they were doing and listened. One said in his broken English, "It came from in there, somewhere!"

Another one said, "I thought all the phones would be disconnected!"

J.C. had locked the door from inside with the old rusty key that had been stuck in the door. Just as the doorknob moved, Missy had reached her phone, and shut it off. They stood dead silent as the men tried to pry the door open. J.C. thought, evidently they don't have another key for the lock. That was a break for them!

The French guy said, "I know I heard something ring, and it came from inside that room!" They then spotted a phone sitting on an antique piece of furniture, so one went over and picked up the receiver. He smiled, and said, "It is connected. I hear a dial tone."

"So much for ghosts." Said the German, laughing.

So, they went back to the crate, lifted it, and carried it down the corridor toward the docking area.

J.C. slowly opened the door, and taking Missy's hand, they slipped out, staying close to the corridor wall. It was dimly lit, causing shadows that kept them alert to any movement. They followed the path the robbers had taken, staying far enough back not to be discovered. Arriving at the servant's entrance, they slowly cracked open the door. No sign of the robbers. Cautiously they crept toward the cave entrance, avoiding the three men who were now struggling to board their stolen goods on the beached boat J.C. and Missy had observed earlier. Hidden in the tall dense brush bordering both sides of the waterway, they continued to creep towards their destination—the cave in the near mountainside.

Missy stopped, and J.C., following close behind, was confused why she had stopped. She removed her cell phone, and, turning it on, dialed her parents number, but it would not ring. She wanted to leave a message telling them where they were, but their phone was not receiving a thing. So, she turned it off again. She sure didn't want a repeat performance and alert these robbers to their escape.

J.C picked up a jagged rock, lying by the edge of the brush. In case they were confronted, he wanted something to try and protect them with. From now on, there would be no hiding places. If the bandits suddenly discovered they had been found out, they might come after them.

With a fluttering of wings, and a loud squawk, a large pheasant jumped out of the brush and took flight in front of Missy. She let out a gasp, but J.C. quickly put his hand over her mouth, preventing her from screaming aloud. Luck wasn't on their side this time however. The sudden gasp and muffled scream had been enough to alert the smugglers.

The men were busy lifting the heavy crate into the boat when one of them stopped, put his finger to his mouth, and said to the others, "Shhhh.... Did you hear something?" The others looked around, but heard nothing.

J.C. and Missy were within shouting distance, standing close together, not making a sound. They had to somehow get around the three men to reach their destination, the cave.

The men continued on, and scooted the crate over to make room to load the other ones.

"I'm going to make a diversion. As soon as I start running, you keep right up with me!" J.C. said, looking at Missy seriously.

She nodded yes.

When the men sat down to rest, J.C. threw the rock as far as he could, out toward the water. It bounced off the tree stump where the boat was anchored, into the water. The men jumped to their feet, and looked over that way.

J.C. grabbed Missy by the hand, and ran across the open area as fast as they could go, then kept on running. The men looked their way, shouting, took their guns from their holsters, and started to run after them.

Finally, after what seemed like hours instead of minutes, they broke from the bright sunlight into the foreboding gloom of the cave. Moving swiftly, yet cautiously, they clung together trying to get a sense of direction.

Then a thought came to J.C. "I sure hope this is the same way we entered! If we're in one of those tunnels going off in other directions we could get trapped and caught."

Missy was slowing, wearing down, but J.C. urged, "You can't stop now, Missy! Keep going!"

As he looked back, he could see the men hadn't given up but were fast gaining on them. He was practically dragging Missy as she was crying, saying, "Go on J.C., and get help! I can't keep up any longer!"

He stopped a moment and shouted, "You can't stop!! I'm not leaving you!"

Suddenly J.C. felt a tug on the neck of his shirt, and just as suddenly, total darkness.

"Missy, are you there!" J.C. exclaimed.

Missy whispered, "Yes, J.C., I can't see a thing."

J.C. took her hand. "Where are we? What happened? What happened to the robbers?"

Missy, so frightened she could hear her heart pounding, replied, "I don't know. It…it felt like something grabbed us, and then we went through the wall…. or the wall opened up and closed again."

"I can't see a thing either," Exclaimed J.C. "Turn on your cell phone Missy, so we'll be able to see from the lighted screen." Unfortunately, by this time the batteries had gone dead, along with their hopes for light.

"You have any matches on you, J.C.?" Missy asked hopefully.

Happily J.C. felt in his pocket and came out with some he had picked up at the coffee shop that morning to take for a souvenir. Striking one, they jumped back against the wall—with eyes wide open, and mouths that could not make a sound, from the sight before them. Skeletons!! They were standing in a buried tomb!

Above them was an old rack with a torch in it. J.C. took it out, and tried to light it. But, it was so old the oil must have dried up. Match after match J.C. continued to strike, but the old torch would not light. Finally, with hope all but gone, it took hold and ignited. Slowly at first and then with an ember as bright as the sun. They stepped cautiously over the bones, feeling along the wall to see if they could find the secret entrance that had snatched them up.

"It has to be here somewhere!" J.C. said, getting agitated that he couldn't find where the secret entrance had been. He kept on feeling, trying and find a break in the wall. Something had to have moved or swiveled for them to have left the cave entrance. Thankfully, he heard no sounds of pursuit from the smugglers on their trail.

Missy touched J.C. on the shoulder, pointing to a wooden door at the far end of the tomb. They moved over to it, and found it was locked from the outside. Leaning up against the wall, their breathing was getting noticeably heavy, and knowing oxygen was limited in here, he knew he would have to find a way out—or they would die in here, probably never to be found.

Missy said, "Listen! I hear water!" They put their ears to the door, and it sounded like a great rushing force of water just outside the door.

J.C. told Missy to step aside. He took a running leap, and with his shoulder, he hit the door with everything he had, and fell to the floor! His shoulder ached, but he knew he could not give up. The door was so old the wood had started to decay. With force, it should give way! He stood up and tried again, and again. Falling to the floor once more, he held his shoulder and sobbed in frustration.

"It's no use Missy. No matter how many times I hit the door, it just won't budge."

Missy came to his side, and put her arms around him, saying, "Don't worry, J.C., somehow we will find a way out." She then tip-toed around the skeletons back to the spot they miraculously fell in, and slid her hand around, feeling for open cracks or hinges, proof of a hidden door. Her torch began burning out, and darkness was beginning to engulf them again. She prayed silently, "Dear Lord, please find us a way to escape, and soon!"

Slowly the two youngsters sank to the ground, along with their hopes. As the last of the torch flickered and went out, total darkness engulfed the pair once more. It would take a miracle now. Maybe what or whoever had gotten them to this place, would get them out. J.C. didn't want to cry in front of Missy, but if there ever was a time, this sure felt like it. He could hear her breathing now beginning to labor, as well as his own. Slowly he reached out and slipped his arm around Missy's shoulders. She in turn took his hand in hers. Together, they waited for the inevitable.

A sound....it started out like a faint creak, then slowly became louder. Suddenly, it felt like a giant earthquake as the walls seemed to shake around them. They heard a huge crash, then a splash, and moonlight was shining down on them. A cold gust of wind hit them full force preventing them from rising. Then, just as suddenly, it stopped! Now the silence was broken by the sound of a waterfall cascading down the side of a mountain.

They could not believe it. The old wooden door had given way, apparently on it's own, letting in fresh, cool air, and moonbeams were now flooding in, giving them light.

"How could the door just cave-in like that?!" Exclaimed J.C. "I couldn't budge it when I tried."

"Maybe it was old and the wind just blew it down at that moment. Or, maybe, it was the answer to our prayer. Whatever it was, we couldn't have done it without the help." Missy surmised.

They walked to the door and started to step out, but, J.C. shouted, "STOP!!" Grabbing Missy, holding her back—before them was a drop-off—with no visible bottom! In front of them was the gigantic waterfall they had heard, partly frozen.

J.C. looked down and around, and all he could see was a steep, smooth cliff—straight down—and hundreds of fir trees. The snow was falling, it was such a beautiful sight, but, he was thinking, just how could they ever get down and find a trail to get back to the others!? Surely, they would have searchers out trying to find them by now. But, they would have no idea which side of the mountain they were on! He wasn't even sure, now, what side they had come out on.

Missy took her cell phone out again. Maybe the batteries had rejuvenated enough to make one last call. She looked at it hoping against hope that it would actually work this time. She turned it on, punched in her mom's number and waited. A weak ring tone...then..., she heard her mother's voice, crying, "Hello! Hello! Is that you, Missy?"

Missy started crying, "Mother! Yes, it's me!" They were both crying now.

"Where on earth are you?" Margery questioned.

"We don't know. Somewhere inside an old tomb." Missy went on to explain, and tell her about the criminals and their guns, "We are way up high in the castle, overlooking the cliff, standing in a door opening that drops down a huge ravine and giant waterfall, just outside the castle! MOM!! PLEASE GET US OUT OF HERE!!!

"You two stay there!" She demanded. "I'm going to call your father. He has a search team out looking for both of you up around the front side of the castle. Just stay where you're at, and don't move! We will come to get you." Then she hung up the phone.

Missy sighed, feeling a little better since she had finally gotten through to her mother, and knowing they would soon be rescued. She looked down at her feet, and there, coming straight for them were—rats!! She let out a blood curdling scream, and J.C. about jumped out of his hide!

"What is the matter with you!?" He said, turning in her direction, not noticing what looked to be hundreds of rats coming out from under the bones scattered everywhere.

She ran over to him, and was practically in his arms as the rats came even closer. Looking down, coming straight for them were more rats than they'd ever seen in their lives.

"I'm leaving! I don't know how, but I'm getting out of here!" She shouted.

J.C. knew he had to think of some way for them to escape—and think of it FAST!

J.C. asked, "You know how to climb down trees, don't you?"

She whimpered back, "No."

He responded, "Well, you're about to have your first lesson. You see that big branch hanging out from that cedar tree?" She looked out the opening, and said, "Yes."

"Well, I'm going to jump on that branch, then I want you to do the same. Follow everything that I do." He said, emphatically. Giving her instructions, he had an idea how to get to the bottom, but it would be very dangerous. He took a leap, and grabbed hold of the sturdy branch. It was slick from the mist of the waterfall and snow, so he wiped it off as much as he could, and shouted back to her, "Now, do what I did, Missy!"

She was more than afraid, knowing that with one slip she could fall to her death instantly. "No! I can't do it!! I'm too afraid!" She said, trembling and holding on tight to the door frame.

He knew she had to conquer her fear, or die there. "Missy, jump and I will grab you. It is either this or the rats! Which will it be!?"

Looking in back of her, the rats were still gathering and advancing toward her. Tears falling on her cheeks, she knew she had to do it. She took a deep breath, then a giant leap, and J.C. caught her in his arms. She hung onto him tightly and sobbed. With great relief, he held her, and said with a grin, "I think you're going to be a champion tree climber after all!"

Also relieved, she smiled then, and stopped crying. Then they both had to laugh because J.C. could always cheer her up. That was one of the things she loved about him.

Slowly, cautiously they descended down the huge, old tree till they got over to a narrow piece of ground. Below them was a creek with a swift current. J.C. jumped down on the ground, and Missy followed him. Now they found themselves on a very narrow trail winding down toward the foot of the castle. They stopped for a moment and she tried calling her mother. The phone was definitely dead this time.

They continued on and came to an opening in the trees. They looked over, and there, standing stately and tall, was the back side of the castle. As they proceeded, now and then they would see a faint light, possibly flashlights of scarchers looking for them. Or, they shuddered to think, could they be the smugglers?

After going as far as they could go before total darkness engulfed them, J.C. suggested they rest. He found a spot under the cliff, and they sat down on the cold and wet ground. J.C. put his arms around her to keep her warm, and soon Missy fell asleep, leaning against his shoulder.

Chapter 15

"A Family Reunion."

The first light of day shone through the thick branches of the cedar trees. Jake, Stu, and Luke, with a search team of many, caught the criminals as they were trying to get away on the boat. The authorities had them locked up now.

The evening before, Horace had someone drive the van with the women back to the hotel, for it was bitterly cold. The search team finally had to give up because in the snow and darkness they were not able to see their feet before them. They had promised to return with the first light to find the secret crypt where, supposedly, the kids spent the night. Margery was very concerned when she could not get them to answer their phone, thinking the phone's battery probably went dead, and they must be very cold.

They were gathering rope and additional supplies they would need; climbing gear to scale the cliff wall on the side where the waterfall was. This was the last place they knew the kids had been before vanishing again. Luke was packing a thermos of hot coffee and snacks. Jake was hugging Moreen and his kids, promising to be careful. Stu was in the van, ready to head back up the mountain, when they spotted the constable's car coming up the street and park. The door flew open, and out ran Missy into the arms of her parents. J.C. was hesitant. He stood back, feeling guilty, that it was all his fault for getting Missy in such a mess that could have proven fatal.

Sylvia hurried over to J.C. and put her arms around him. "Oh, J.C., we have been so worried about you two!"

Horace followed her, saying, "Where have you been son? Everyone has been out searching all night."

J.C. was choked up, so he just shrugged his shoulders and looked down at the ground. Missy whispered, "Dad, go easy on J.C. He saved my life!"

Luke walked over, and J.C. kept his eyes down at the ground. He wouldn't look him in the face, knowing Missy's parents thought the worst of him now, that he was not a responsible man. But, Luke put his arms around him, saying, "Son, how can I ever thank you enough? Missy told me some of the things you two endured, and she thinks pretty highly of you."

J.C. looked him in the face, and said, "I'm sorry Luke. If it hadn't been for me talking her into going inside the castle, none of this would have happened." His eyes moistened again.

Sylvia held him, saying, "You mustn't think that way. You kids were just exploring, having a good time. How could you have ever predicted there would be dangerous men in there robbing the place?"

Luke added, "J.C., you and Missy will probably get a reward. Those men were very dangerous, and had been doing this kind of thing a long time, evading the authorities. Who'd figure that two kids would be responsible for their discovery?"

Sylvia told them to come along and clean up, and have some

breakfast because they needed to be heading out for Oberammergau. As they loaded the van down again with the luggage, Sylvia reminded Horace, "Don't forget, Hon, we have to take a wooden souvenir back home, and find out where your ancestors had lived outside of Oberammergau." Another adventure ended....a new one to begin.

Chapter 16

"The Town."

Wood carving was Horace's ancestors' way of making a living. It's an ancient art practice in Oberammergau (there's even a couple of schools in town that teach it.) The desk clerk had informed them a usual oberammergau souvenir would be a wooden crucifix.

"Also, while you're in Bavaria," The desk clerk went on," You should purchase a handmade clock! There are two kinds of wooden clocks that can be purchased. The first is a coo coo clock, which may vary in size and price, and the second one is a Bavarian clock. In Bavaria the clocks run differently; they go in the opposite direction of conventional clocks, and have the inscription, *In Bayern gehen die uhren anders. Bayern* means Bavaria, *gehen die or doch* means clock, *uhren* means runs, and *anders* means different. So it means, 'In Bavaria the clocks run different. My cousin has a clock shop down town in Oberammergau. Just down the street from where you will be staying. Tell him I sent you."

She had phoned ahead and made reservations for the group, and they were so grateful.

The desk clerk went on, " For a small town, Oberammergau offers a great variety of places to eat. If you don't wish to spend too much money on food, you can try eating at an imbiss (bars in which food is also served). You can also eat at one of the many hotels or guest houses (where international food and local food is served). There are many varieties of food to choose from. For instance you can eat some of the best burgers in Charlie's Imbiss or, if you're in the mood, you should try a mexican restaurant. Desserts are to be found, not only in the restaurants, but also in some cafes. Hot beverages are served in the small cafes in town. There are also Cafe/Ice shops in which coffee and ice creams are sold all year round. But, if you'd like to have a nightcap, then you probably would want to go to some of the town's bars."

Horace and the men were planning on doing just that, after the woman folk retired back at the hotel that evening. A mug of warm German beer would hit the spot after such a long, eventful day.

Everyone was lining up as Hilda made a head count. Missy and J.C. were the last to show up, for they were talking to the desk clerk, along with a few of her cousins, wanting to know where they could have fun among young people. They all agreed on going to the Kino Cafe (a movie theater with a cafe) for a couple of hours.

"In there, you're most likely to find any kind of cocktail you want, and also some good food. But if you want to experience some of the local folklore, then Zum Tonis is the right place for you." Said the receptionist at the hotel desk. "It's a typical Bavarian bar, with a friendly staff and a large variety of local and international schnapps."

Sylvia overheard the conversation. "Oh, no, no, NO!" She said. "A movie, yes. But no German Schnapps for you, yet! You're still too young!"

The receptionist continued, "For such a small town, Oberammergau offers quite a variety of hotels, with prices between 45 euros to 200 euros per night. Location is really irrelevant since the town is quite small. Some of the hotels are pretty basic in what they offer. You can stay in places like bed and breakfasts, which are more "family oriented," or you can stay at a 5 star hotel like Maximilian Hotel. You may want to consider which hotel is adequate to your needs, like if you're traveling alone, or if you're bringing children or pets, for some hotels are more suitable than others. For backpacking travelers there is the local Youth Hostel. I know you will like the one we booked you in, but if not there are a lot of other choices. Good-bye, and have a very good time!" She said, handing Sylvia her receipt.

Moreen yelled out to Jake, "Everyone's accounted for! We are ready to go!" Jake pulled out, and headed for the highway and open road. The trip to Oberammergau was beautiful. The scenery kept them enthralled, and their cameras filming. It seemed like no time till they exited off into the small town.

Jake drove into the main part of town and was greeted by a huge fir tree, decorated up with fruit and popcorn for the winter birds to eat. They parked and gazed out on this quaint, but elegant little town, with delicately painted murals on the sides of all the small shops. It was as if they were looking into a different world, so simple and lovely as the snow was falling on this story-book setting. Jake got out and asked for directions to the Ferienhaus Fux Hotel, near downtown and within walking distance of everything. Luftmalerei mural paintings could be found on just about every building, making the illusion of being mystical, like a fairyland.

Driving up to the front entrance, everyone got out and checked in. Jake parked the van because everything seemed to be just what they'd hoped—within walking distance. They ate a lunch at the hotel restaurant, then bundling up warm to go strolling along the narrow streets, window shopping—a thing Horace and Sylvia used to do way back when they were first married. Back then, money wasn't too plentiful, and it was a fun way to pass a Sunday evening, peering through the decorated storefront windows, dreaming of what they would buy if they only had the money.

The snow was trickling down, and it sure looked, and felt like, they had stepped inside a storybook with the sights and sounds of a Charles Dickens Christmas Holiday.

Chapter 17

"Sharing The Christmas Spirit in Fairyland."

April and Harry went with Moreen and her family over to a soda shop. Horace and Sylvia stopped and had a relaxing, steaming cup of hot chocolate at a small cafe, and then Sylvia joined up with the rest of the woman and small children and headed back to their hotel to rest. It had been an exceptionally, enjoyable day.

The men strolled on down to the local pub to visit and relax before retiring. As Sylvia got them ready for bed, April and Harry could not stop talking about Santa Claus.

"Does Santa Claus live here?" Harry asked, "Here in Ober….Ober…amer." Having difficulty pronouncing the name.

Sylvia laughed, and enunciated the syllables of the name very slowly so he could sound them out. Then she said, "Santa Claus lives at the North Pole, but on Christmas Eve he travels every inch of the world, delivering gifts to every boy and girl."

April spoke up, "Boys and girls like us?"

Sylvia smiled, thinking how sad it was that they had never enjoyed a Christmas before. Santa had never came to them because they were constantly on the road. Now, they seemed to think they were different than other children. Tucking them in and giving each a good night kiss, she was thinking to herself, Horace and I have got to make this Christmas memorable, the very best one they have ever had, for those kids have never even experienced love.

Then a negative thought came to her—wonder what if they are taken from us, and we'd never see them again? She dismissed that thought immediately! Then quickly answered, "Yes, boys and girls just like you and Harry!" They gave her those special smiles that warmed her heart every time. As she turned off the light and closed the door behind her she heard their tiny voices saying, "Good-night, Mrs. D."

After taking a nice hot shower, she picked up a book and started reading. After a while she pulled the chair over by the window and watched the beautiful snow falling down on the sleepy, scenic little village of Oberammergau.

Sylvia was fast asleep when Horace came to bed. In the short time he had been here, he was already madly in love with the city of his ancestors. The warm German Schnapps and good camaraderie with family made him feel so relaxed, ready for a good night's sleep. He leaned over and gave his wife a goodnight kiss, lightly, for she was sound asleep, snoring and already in dreamland.

Morning came, and the awesome scenery outside their window in this beautiful little valley snuggled in between the Alps brought back the Christmas spirit in full force! The little town was all decorated for Jesus' birthday party. The buildings were painted with frescoes, murals, and smiling people full of Christmas joy were already moving around.

Sylvia watched, from the window, a group of children running with sleds. Some were darting into the small Italian ice cream shop for a treat. She chuckled to herself, thinking, probably their parents didn't know they were having ice cream so early in the morning. She spotted a tiny bakery shop, and she envisioned a big tray, full of the delicious Bavarian pastry. The snow had ceased during the night, but plenty was left for skiers up on Laber Mountain.

Hearing Horace, Sylvia sat down at the table with him over a steaming hot cup of coffee, compliments of the hotel. They exchanged good mornings and the usual conversation they had every morning, then Sylvia suggested getting dressed while he finished off his coffee. Horace suggested she get some pastries, since both of them had a sweet tooth, so she slipped over to the bakery for a box of goodies to munch on through the day.

When she returned, placing the delicacies on the small table, she asked, "What are you doing?" He handed her a pamphlet, and she read, "Oberammergau is most famous for the Passion Play," Then pausing, said disappointingly, "But, it's performed in October."

Horace leaned back in his chair reminiscing about stories about this place told to him by Grandpa Deterding, long ago when he was a child. "You know, his folks were in that play?!" It made him feel that a piece of him had always been here, just waiting to be discovered.

Sylvia went on reading the rest. Horace listened, then said, "How interesting. The Passion Play will be performing again in nine years." Then looking over the table at her, he said, "If we are still around, I was thinking, maybe we can return for it?"

She smiled warmly, and said, "We will make it a point to be here then!"

That morning they walked around admiring the beautiful, exquisite, tiny shops with wood carving displays. This craft was important to this area having been inherited through generations. Wood carving has been, still is, traditional family businesses, around these parts, since the Middle Ages. This has also contributed to

Oberammergau's popularity, along with the fantastic scenic countryside with miles of hiking trails and cycle tracks that give you unique, spectacular, panoramic views of the beautiful surrounding scenery. Hikers and mountain climbers come to explore the Kofel, the local mountain of Oberammergau, or take the chairlift to the Kolben, or the cable lift to the Laber Mountain. From the peaks one can enjoy a picture postcard, spectacular view of the famous Old Wies Church, along with King Ludwig's Land with it's fairy tale castles, Neuschwanstein and Linderhof. As Horace took notice of this, he thought to himself, I think we have had our share of castle adventures for one trip.

Sylvia and Horace stood by the bus as the family gathered, trying to decide where to go first. Sylvia cleared her throat, hoping to get Horace's attention. "Horace!" She called to him, but he was still basking in his thoughts, absorbed in the beauty around him. He didn't hear his wife's voice at all.

"Horace!" She said a little bit louder. He raised his head, looking at her over his Ben Franklin glasses.

"The children have been asking to go snowmobiling or skiing.... The girls thought it would be fun to take them up on the Kolben area where they have runs for beginners and intermediates."

Horace smiled, saying, "Does that mean I have to wear training wheels!?"

She laughed, "Yes. We would like to have a picture of you with training wheels on your skis, and a big pillow strapped on your behind, skiing down a mountain here! Wouldn't that make a fine photo on all our Christmas cards?!"

He raised his paper cup of hot coffee to her, and answered, "Cheers!" And then added, "Did you bring the remainder of those sweets you bought in the bakery shop, or did you leave them back in our room?"

She laughed, and held her paper cup of coffee up to him, saying, sweetly, "Ich bring dir!" (meaning, "I bring it to you.")

He grinned at her attempt at the German language.

"I believe you took too much part in the "trinken" (means drink in German) last night with the boys, my dear Horace. You need more coffee?" Sylvia said, teasing her husband a bit because she did not believe in the consumption of alcohol of any sorts. Her Southern Baptist upbringing had taught her to stand firm on these issues.

He raised his coffee cup again and smiled, "Cheers!" But he was feeling the after-affects. The pain felt like a sledge hammer banging in his head, and would soon call for an aspirin for sure. He had even killed the noise of the ticking coo coo clock hanging on the wall that morning, for it sounded like Big Ben clanging in his ears. Not one to indulge in alcoholic beverages, Horace none-the-less couldn't withstand the temptation of having a mug of stout, warm German beer enjoyed in an authentic pub while he was here.

Sylvia and Horace boarded the bus, and found a seat. She took from her purse the aspirin bottle and handed it to him, with the thermos bottle of water. As they rode along, they enjoyed the uniquely beautiful scenery, the old cathedral, and old Lahn Bridge.

Horace mumbled to himself, "Sightseeing. Now this is more my speed. Not skiing! Training wheels on my skis?" Chuckling at the thoughts.

They had taken in, and learned a lot, in the short time they had been here. They found out the Holidays in the Ammergauer Alps are magical this time of year. The Ammergauer Alps are located between Germany's highest mountain, the Zugspitze, and the famous castle Neuschwanstein, in the heart of the Bavarian Alps. Now they were headed for the small town of Unterammergau, called

"Kinderlandort." Located next to mountain Steckenberg, and being children friendly, it would offer fun for the whole family. Sledding, ice-skating, Nordic-walking, or snowshoeing. When the ice is thick enough, Lake Soier, is the most beautiful location for ice skating and curling. Also in Oberammergau, they could try these sports at the Malensteinweg (a popular street in town.)

Chapter 18

"A Shopping Excursion."

The bus stopped, and April and Harry came running. They were the first ones off. When Sylvia stepped off, they grabbed her around her legs, jumping up and down with excitement, and then went to Horace eager to get going and have fun, seeing the sights and experiencing all there was here on the mountain.

"Mr. D., what are we going to see today!" They asked. He laughed, and hugged them, saying, "Well, we've got lots of choices, but a little bird told me you two wanted to ski."

They clapped and cheered, "Mr. D., you going with us, too!?"

Horace shook his head, no, "I'm getting too old for that sort of thing. But, I will sit in the nice warm lodge and watch you."

They looked at him questioning, "Who could see us skiing, sitting inside the lodge?!"

So, April and Harry went with Luke and his family, along with J.C. and the others to go skiing. Horace and Sylvia decided on a leisurely walk around town and a quiet lunch.

Christmas Eve would come tomorrow, and they still had

shopping to do. And, Horace wanted so to find the farm his ancestors had left, sailing to America and a new life. Sylvia was looking for the perfect doll for April. She had never had a new doll. Sylvia and Horace peered into the window of the small toy shop in the small mountain village and the beautiful porcelain dolls. A tiny train set was set up and moving right along around the decorated Christmas tree, and a sign caught her eye "BAVARIAN FAIRY TALE CHRISTMAS."

"Yes!" She said to Horace. "This certainly is our Bavarian Fairy Tale Christmas!" She took out her camera, and started taking pictures of everything she could see through the lens. "When we get home, I'm going to collect every picture and film from everyone, and make up a DVD for each family; a remembrance of our wonderful Bavarian Fairy Tale Christmas."

They had taken much film of The Castle of Neuschwanstein, built by King Ludwig. It had been used for many movies, and the beauty of the area was known world-wide as a fantasyland. And, at Christmas time, when the villages, forests and mountains were covered with a blanket of snow, it transforms into a magnificent, winter wonderland, white Christmas."

Sylvia and Horace bought April's gifts from a quaint little doll shop. Now it was time to find Harry a German-made bear and the tiny little train. Also, for J.C., they bought a case of various knives, including a Bowie knife, for he had taken an interest in the old craft of wood carving. Hopefully, if everything worked out as planned, he would be the one to carry on the tradition. Also, a beautiful, hand-knit sweater would be something J.C. could use.

That day proved out a success for everyone. They boarded the bus and hurried back to their hotel rooms. Sylvia had to figure out how to keep the kids (April, Harry, and J.C.) busy so she could wrap the gifts before they returned. Sylvia had stopped at the pastry shop, again, and got two of everything. Horace picked up a table-top, decorated Christmas tree. They had so much fun decorating their suite and wrapping the packages. They hid them in their bedroom closet to put out late Christmas Eve after the kids went to sleep.

When Luke and Margery brought the kids back, they all were very surprised that Sylvia and Horace had brought a bit of Christmas into their hotel. It reminded them of home. Everyone spent the evening with last-minute shopping and preparations. Later they would wrap their packages and place them around the little tree in Horace and Sylvia's suite.

April and Harry's eyes got large, seeing all the gifts. When they saw some had their names on them, they started asking questions, "Mrs. D.! Did Santa come early!?"

She looked over at Horace for an answer. He picked April up into his lap, and Harry leaned on Horace with big eyes, listening to Horace's explanation of why all these gifts showed up before midnight on Christmas Eve (tomorrow night).

"Well," Horace was thinking fast. What story could he come up with on the spur of the moment?

"Well, you see, Santa came by for a visit to make sure he got everyone's request right, before making his rounds tomorrow night on Christmas Eve. You know he has the whole world to deliver to."

They both looked at each other, surprised. "We missed him!! He came while we were gone!?" April said, almost crying.

"Well, yes and no, April. He will still come late tomorrow night, after you and Harry are sound asleep." Horace wiped her tear away.

Their eyes grew wide, and smiles came over their faces. They hugged Horace, then jumped down, running into their bedroom. Horace and Sylvia grinned at each other as they heard them giggling and whispering, wondering if Santa would bring them something special.

Chapter 19

"Blessings."

That evening, they all gathered outside the hotel. The snow was falling, again, and you could smell the wood burning fireplaces used all over town.

Horace leaned into Sylvia with his arm in hers. "This all reminds me of something out of a Christmas card, don't you think so?"

She smiled, and said, "Yes it does. All we need is carolers singing "Silver Bells, or White Christmas."

About that time, a sleigh hitched to a beautiful dapple grey came around the street corner carrying a couple, and everyone waved at them. Hilda took her cam-corder out and filmed it. Music could be heard up around the city park. The family walked together with a crowd that had gathered near the city's Christmas tree, and stood to watch while the lights were turned on.

They found a nice restaurant, with a fireplace, that would hold them all at once. There, they spent several hours eating, visiting, and singing karaoke Christmas songs. The evening was topped off with a glass of red wine as Horace toasted the family. He toasted the blessings of a large, close-knit family, enjoying a Christmas they would always remember.

Christmas Eve Day! Everyone was sleeping in, tired from the full day before. Sylvia always saw to it they started off their day with a nice, nourishing breakfast. As they entered the lobby they heard the lady at the desk talking about the tour beginning shortly. So, Horace and Sylvia took the kids on the shuttle bus with them while J.C. decided to hang out with Luke and and his family going ice skating. Although J.C didn't have a clue how to skate, they all were going to teach him.

"Our newest White Christmas tour starts here and goes to Frankfurt, then travels to Stuttgart (home of the Mercedes Museum and several great Christmas Markets), then back here to Oberammergau." They heard the tour guide explaining.

"Who knows the name of the capitol city of Bavaria?" She called out, looking around for hands. Harry jumped up and screamed out in a very high pitched voice, "Munich!" Everyone laughed, for he didn't quite get the punctuation right, and it came out, Munshic!

They arrived in Frankfurt, and had a guided, walking tour of the historical centre of Frankfurt. Then they visited the Christmas Advent Markets on the Roemerberg.

Sylvia could smell the tantalizing aromas of burning incense, mulled wine, cinnamon, and gingerbread cookies. They had lunch, a true Bavarian, wonderful meal, then boarded the shuttle bus again, driving south to the Student Prince town of Heidelberg. There, they stopped to visit the Christmas Market on the famous Kornmarkt in central Heidelberg, and visited the castle ruins.

In the afternoon, they continue to Stuttgart and the Mercedes Benz Museum, the Historic town of Augsburg, one of the most important cites on the Romantic Road. After a late meal, they returned to the small village of Oberammergau.

The kids were tuckered out, and had already fallen asleep, lying between Horace and Sylvia. It had been a long, but wonderful, day of sightseeing. As soon as the bus stopped, Sylvia woke the children, and they headed for their hotel room. J.C. was waiting up for them, a little worried because it was so late.

"Off to bed!" Sylvia demanded. April and Harry shuffled off, sleepy eyed and anticipating Santa's arrival.

Sylvia hurried, and with J.C. 's help, got the packages down from the closet, and arranged them around their tree.

Sylvia put her arms around J.C., and said, "Merry Christmas, J.C. We are so blessed to have you, April, and Harry with us. I really hope you are enjoying your holiday."

He hung his head for a moment, and Horace put his arm around him. "There something wrong, Son?"

J.C. started tearing up, and, in a whisper, he said, "I wish Santa could make you our parents for good."

Horace held him as he looked into Sylvia's eyes, also full of tears.

"Well, Son," Horace said softly. "We just have to give it all over to the Lord, and hope for the best."

As Horace and Sylvia got ready for bed that night, they knew in their hearts this was one Christmas they never would forget.

Chapter 20

"Presents."

April woke up first. Then she slipped out of bed and went over to Harry's bed, and woke him up. The sun was just coming up over the mountains as they quietly opened the bedroom door and slipped past J.C., asleep on the living room sofa. The tree was lit, and they had never in their lives seen such a sight—so many presents! Harry whispered, "Can we look and see if Santa left us something?"

They kneeled down and found a gift, "To April." She picked it up and slightly shook it. They wanted so to open them because the suspense was killing them!

"You want to see what Santa brought you!?" Came a voice from behind that almost scared them out of their wits! They stood up, and looked at her, afraid they had done something wrong. There stood Sylvia in her long granny nightgown.

She hugged them and whispered, "Well, okay. If you really want to see what Santa brought, go to it! Make sure they have your names on them first before ripping the paper off!"

Sylvia smiled and walked into the kitchenette to put the coffee on.

Taking a big box of homemade donuts from the bakery out of the frig and placing them on the table, she glanced back expecting a whirlwind of papers and ribbons to be flying in the air. But, to her surprise, the children had folded the wrapping paper and put the bows into a neat pile. It was as if the outsides of the gifts were as precious to them as what was inside.

Hearing the excited giggling, J.C. rolled over and yawned, trying to focus in on what was happening. Soon Horace opened the bedroom door, standing there barefoot, and tying his old wool robe. He put his house slippers on, and came over to where all the ruckus was going on, laughing at the sight of the two little kids shaking all the boxes after checking the name tags twice before they opened only their own gifts. April squealed loudly when she opened the box with her beautiful doll in it. She held it close, hugging it tightly, showing everyone what Santa had brought her.

Harry was figuring out how to lay the tracks down for his little choo-choo train. Sylvia brought a cup of coffee over to Horace, and asked J.C. if he would like one. He shook his head no, then got down with the kids on the floor to help put the train together.

April brought him some gifts, and he looked over at Horace and Sylvia, wondering if he should open them or not. Horace smiled, motioned for him to go ahead, and said, "Go ahead, Son. Open your Christmas!"

When he saw the beautiful sweater and knife set, a tear rolled down his face. He had never received anything so beautiful, and meaningful in his life.

Sylvia smiled, saying, "Try it on, J.C. Let's see how it fits." He stood up and pulled it on over his pajamas. It fit perfectly. He went over and gave Sylvia a hug. Horace took him by the hand, saying, "You're not too old to hug me too, are you?!"

J.C. knelt down where Horace was sitting, and threw both

his arms around the neck of the dear older man, saying " Thank you too, Mr. D., for the best Christmas ever."

"Santa brought you some more, so get to opening them up!" Horace laughed, enjoying the sight of these kids' first real Christmas.

There was a knock on the door, and in came the whole family, laughing and wishing everyone a Merry Christmas. April ran and showed Hilda her doll, and then they all had to see it. Moreen and Jake were the last ones in, and they brought the first breakfast cart calling for everyone to help themselves. "There's more food coming!" Moreen called out, trying to be heard over all the joyful noises. Everyone was still in their pajamas as they found a place to sit in this now crowded little area.

The children handed the gifts out, and you could hear laughter and joy, just like they were home in their parents' family room. Horace had brought his old book along on their trip. April spotted it lying on the coffee table and handed it to him, asking,

"Mr. D., will you read us a poem from your book?" As he took it, eyes twinkling, smiling at her standing there with bare feet, clutching tightly to her new doll, he said, "If you and your new dolly will help me turn the pages." She smiled and eagerly climbed up on his lap.

Sylvia called out for everyone to settle down and help themselves to the donuts and coffee, "And, there is milk in the frig for the kids. Someone needs to help them with their glasses and pouring it, then let's listen." She instructed as she settled in a chair near Horace.

So, everyone quickly found a comfy spot to settle down and listen to Horace's special treat, a story all except J.C. and his brother and sister, had heard every year, yet never grew tired of. A story of the very first Christmas—"A Special Christmas."

M*any stars shone bright that night with one much brighter than the rest.*
E*ven shepherds tending flocks noticed a star that traveled West.*
R*ealizing it was foretold, three wise men journeyed from afar.*
R*ejoicing angels brought the news of the meaning of that star.*
Y*uletide spirits, joyful singing, all proclaiming a proud event.*

C*hrist is born in Bethlehem, a gift from God, heaven sent.*
"H*osanna," Sang the angels loudly, "Glory to the newborn king!"*
"R*eceive the news with celebration, let all who hear rejoice and sing!"*
I*n a stable, in a manger, lies a miracle of birth.*
S*hepherds gather by his bedside, wise men bring their gifts of Myrrh.*
T*he animals lay strangely quiet, as if a sound would break the spell.*
M*uch more was taking place than even songs of joy could tell.*
A *baby lying in a manger, as innocent as a newborn dove,*
S*oon would give new meaning to the words, "Eternal Hope, Everlasting Love."*
(From the book, "Rhymes And Reasons, Changing Seasons.")

Harry sat on the arm of the recliner next to Horace as April snuggled against his chest. They were thoroughly enjoying the sights and sounds of their very first family Christmas. Luke came in, and handed Horace the phone, saying, "Dad, I think you'd better take this call." His face was serious. What he said next caused the room to suddenly go still. "It's the Judge..."

J.C. quit unwrapping his gifts, and April and Harry climbed down, went over to him, and sat against him. He put his arms around them as they listened to every word being said. Would this be good news...or would it be bad news, instructing them to be placed in another foster home?

Horace took the receiver and said, "Hello, Judge. I thought we had till January second for the court date." Then he listened to what the Judge was saying, never smiling, or saying anything to indicate what was being said to him. He ended the conversation with, "Merry Christmas to you, Judge. And, to your family, as well!"

Everyone's eyes were on Horace. Sylvia was wiping away a tear, silently praying hard for good news. When Horace motioned for the kids to come over to him, J.C's heart fell. He just knew they would be taken by Child and Family Services as soon as they returned to the States. April and Harry came over to him, and he lifted them up on his lap. Horace spoke loud and clearly, for everyone to hear, "Family, I want you to meet your new sister and brothers!!"

The cheers went up and hands were clapping. Tabitha picked up April and swung her around, singing, "I have a little sister! I have a little brother, and a big one, too!" Then she grabbed Harry, and everyone in the family took turns hugging, kissing, and wishing everyone a very happy holiday. Luke's daughter was the first to come over to J.C., and hug him. Tears were streaming down his face, and hers, too, for he could not believe what he was hearing.

Sylvia lifted her arms up to Heaven and said a prayer, thanking God for His divine intervention. She leaned in and asked Horace, "What happened to those people who were wanting the kids?"

Horace whispered back, "They backed out. After rethinking it, they thought the kids would be happier with us, and not separated. The Judge couldn't wait to tell us when we came back. He thought it would be a great Christmas gift to call us from his home."

Sylvia hugged Horace, and he gave her a warm kiss. Hilda reached for a sprig of mistletoe, and held it up for her parents' Christmas kiss. That Sunday, they all attended church service in Oberammergau, and gave thanks to a God that is gracious and full of love.

Chapter 21

"Home Of My Ancestors."

Monday morning, Horace inquired around and found his ancestors' old place just outside of town. Jake drove the family out there, and in the shadows of the mountain range they found nothing left but pasture land. They all stood there on the same ground their ancestors of yesteryear had lived out their lives, and some who had left to find a new life in far away America. They looked around and took photographs. It was a lovely place, and Horace thought to himself, it would have taken a lot of gumption for them to uproot and leave here, sailing across a treacherous sea to a land they knew nothing about.

They all got back in the van, and were driving a short way down the road when someone cried, "STOP—LOOK!" There on a small, thatched roof cottage was a tiny sign that simply read, "DETERDING."

Luke drove up the narrow lane and got out. He walked over to the front door, and on a homemade bench next to the door was painted, "Velcome." He knocked gently. A few moments passed. Then, just as he was about to leave, the door slowly opened, and standing there was a very short, tiny lady. Her hair was gray, and combed up into a bun on the top of her head.

"Who is at my door? Please identify yourself." She asked.

Luke could tell she could not see very well, as he held his hand out to hers, and replied, "Hello, Madam. My name is Luke Deterding. I'm from America. My ancestors lived on the land next to yours." He paused a moment, then went on, "Seeing the name Deterding over your door, well, I was hoping you and I might be related from way back, somehow." He noticed she had the sweetest smile as she opened her door for him to enter, saying, "Oh, what a pleasant surprise. My late husband was named Luke."

Luke hesitated and then said, "Mrs. Deterding, I have my parents and sisters…well, I have a van outside, full of my family members!"

She laughed and exclaimed, "I am Adela. Please tell them all to come in! It might be crowded, but we will find room."

Luke signaled for the others to join them. They all crowded into her quaint cottage's parlor and made all the introductions of how they were related to each other.

"I have some fresh homemade cookies on the table. Please, you're velcome to them!" Adela invited. But, they declined, saying they only had a short time left to visit, but had wanted to meet her, and see if she could tell them a little more about their roots here in Oberammergau.

The old lady sat down in her small rocking chair, cushioned with pillows they'd bet she made herself. She began by asking where in America they lived, and just what did they already know about the old folks who went there and settled in the 1850's?

After listening to their accounts, she told them, in near perfect English, that she was close to 100 years old. Her husband worked this land until he died suddenly from heart failure. They had one son born to them, but he had drowned in the Rhine

River one summer day when he was only three. She was the last one left of her family. She could not see too well from the cataracts, but was still able to move around to get her housework done, and tend to her garden.

Adela asked how long they had been here, and then turned to little April, asking, "Do you know what Ober-ammer-gau means, child?" Before April could say anything, Harry shouted out, "Upper river valley!"

The tiny woman laughed, waving for the boy to come closer, so she could see him better, saying, "Now, just where did you learn that, Little Boy?"

Harry shuffled over near her, staring in her face, and answered, "Well, Mr. D. told me." Then, smiling, he looked over at Horace, and slowly corrected his sentence, "I mean, my dad told me!" Pointing to Horace, who had a grin from ear to ear.

She smiled at him and said, "What a handsome lad!" His face turned bright red, but he told her that this was the best Christmas they'd ever had, because he, his little sister, and big brother had just been adopted by Mr. and Mrs. D.

Missy told her about their harrowing experience in Mad Max Ludwig's castle, then she suddenly fell silent.... Her voice got quieter and they had to listen close to hear what she said next, "Oh, you know, he wasn't really mad at all. It was others who conspired to blacken his name. You know he was murdered? It is said, his ghost still roams. I've not seen his spirit, myself, but I know ones who swore they have."

She was silent for a moment, then continued with her history of the castle, "He just about broke the nation back then, when he lived, with his eccentric ways, spending foolishly. But, now, just look at how many people, since then, have enjoyed his magnificent castles—and will till the end of time!"

After a moment, Adela went on, "You know, Missy, he is a descendent of ours. I would be almost certain he sensed your danger, and was the one who saved you and J.C., somehow. Pulling you through the secret door into the crypt, and then managing to break through the barrier behind the waterfall was an event surely beyond human means. You know there are many mysteries and miracles hidden in these hills and valleys, a ghost in a cave or divine intervention, who can say. One thing I do know is the secrets of the past and the dreams of the future all come together here."

Suddenly a smile came to Adela's face. "Enough of seriousness! Let me tell you of beautiful things."

She told them of a place that had the best melt-in-your-mouth, cream-laden cakes. Then told them, "Too bad it's not summer so you could enjoy the beautiful flower gardens, and ride down the Rhine River. Just a short walk from town you will find the gondola that takes you up the mountain so you can see our beautiful Bavarian Valley below.

She asked if their accommodations at the hotel were OK. If they weren't, she said to tell them, "You're related to me, and they will make it right!" Also, she told them, "There are fine guest houses around this area, too, very reasonable in prices."

They asked her where the cemetery was where their ancestors were laid to rest, and she got up slowly, saying, "Wait till I get my jacket, and cane. I will show you. It is within walking distance."

They went out to place flowers on graves that could be found. Again, connecting with their roots of long, long ago.

When the time came to go, they all felt a special connection to Adela Deterding and this place. It would always be a second home to them. They took turns hugging the little old lady, as tears ran

MERRY CHRISTMAS!!

The Ghost (reprise)

Somewhere a cold wind blows,
A door opens, how, no one knows.
My touch, soft, gentile, true, and swift,
Will touch the heart, the spirit lift.
Who saved the children? No one knows.
Somewhere a cold wind blows.

down her weathered old face. Horace held her tightly in his arms, and whispered, "You have family now. We will keep in contact."

Sylvia gave her a hug, and promised they would return again one day. But, in the back of her mind, she knew God would have another plan for this lovely new member of their family before their return.

The week went by very fast. Then, the morning came for them to leave beautiful Oberammergau behind and return home. There were sad faces, along with great anticipation of a wonderful, full life for each and everyone—especially for the three orphans who had found a home-place, surrounded with the love of a wonderful family.

April grew up and moved away, after college, to Colorado, and became a country veterinarian.

Harry became a well-known heart specialist in California.

J.C. married Missy, and, in time, they had a large family. He eventually took over the family farm, and became a devoted husband, father, farmer, and wood-carver. When the holidays came around, the whole family, growing ever larger, never failed to return to their home-place, to Horace and Sylvia who lived long lives. Here they would stay and live out their lives, in this small farming community called Cracker's Bend, in Illinois.

Oh yes, they did return to Oberammergau and attended the Passion Play.